SURVIVORS

SWAMP:
LOUISIANA, 1851

Don't miss any of these survival stories:

SWAMP:
LOUISIANA, 1851

KATHLEEN DUEY
and KAREN A. BALE

Aladdin

New York   London   Toronto   Sydney   New Delhi

This book is a work of fiction. Any references to historical events, real people, or real places are used
fictitiously. Other names, characters, places, and events are products of the author's imagination, and
any resemblance to actual events or places or persons, living or dead, is entirely coincidental.

ALADDIN

An imprint of Simon & Schuster Children's Publishing Division

1230 Avenue of the Americas, New York, New York 10020

This Aladdin paperback edition July 2016

Text copyright © 1999 by Kathleen Duey and Karen A. Bale

Cover illustration copyright © 2016 by David Palumbo

Also available in an Aladdin hardcover edition.

All rights reserved, including the right of reproduction in whole or in part in any form.

ALADDIN is a trademark of Simon & Schuster, Inc., and related logo

is a registered trademark of Simon & Schuster, Inc.

For information about special discounts for bulk purchases, please contact

Simon & Schuster Special Sales at 1-866-506-1949 or business@simonandschuster.com.

The Simon & Schuster Speakers Bureau can bring authors to your live event.

For more information or to book an event contact the Simon & Schuster Speakers Bureau

at 1-866-248-3049 or visit our website at www.simonspeakers.com.

Cover designed by Laura DiSiena

Interior designed by Tom Daly

The text of this book was set in Berling LT Std.

Manufactured in the United States of America 0616 OFF

2 4 6 8 10 9 7 5 3 1

Library of Congress Control Number 99-35217

ISBN 978-1-4814-2784-5 (hc)

ISBN 978-1-4814-2783-8 (pbk)

ISBN 978-1-4814-2785-2 (eBook)

For the women
who taught us the meaning of courage:
Erma L. Kosanovich
Katherine B. Bale
Mary E. Peery

SURVIVORS

SWAMP:
LOUISIANA, 1851

Chapter One

The harsh squawk of a crow made Lily LeGrand look up. The long, wooden dye-paddle in her hands came to a stop for a few seconds as she scanned the top of the levee. Where were Augustin and Pierre? If the crows got into the corn now, a week from harvest, Maman would be furious.

Lily started nudging at the cloth again, moving the bolt of cottonade through the simmering liquid. The water reeked of salt and vinegar, the mordants Maman was using to set the dye this time. Staring down into the water, Lily noticed a fleck of onionskin that had somehow missed the strainer.

She bent to pick up a twig and fished out the onionskin, then straightened her back and looked at the sky, wishing she could slip away and paddle her pirogue into the deep reaches of the swamp. It worried Maman when she went, but the truth was, Lily was more comfortable on the water than anywhere else. In her pirogue she was as fleet and graceful as anyone, young or old, man or woman.

Lily sighed. It was going to be another hot morning. They had been having thunderstorms late in the afternoon, and the ground was steaming as the sun rose high enough to clear the line of towering cypress trees on the east side of the bayou.

"Lily!"

The sound of her mother's voice made Lily turn quickly, and she lost her balance, her lame foot refusing to bear her weight. She braced herself against the dye-paddle and managed to avoid falling.

Maman appeared in the doorway as Lily was regaining her footing, then came to the edge of the *gallerie*. She blinked at the glare of the bright sunlight. "Lift the cloth and let me look. I want only a pale yellow for this one."

Lily pushed the paddle deep into the water, winding the cloth around it, then lifted the dripping mass slowly, bracing the end of the paddle against her hip.

"A little longer," Maman said, and Lily lowered the cloth back into the steaming dye bath.

"I heard crows," Lily said.

Her mother pulled in a quick breath and frowned. "Have you seen your brothers?"

Lily shook her head. "But they were out behind the house earlier, fooling around the chickens. Pierre was digging along the back of the *cage à poulet*."

"I asked him to," Maman said. "I want to pour ashes into the ants' nest there—maybe we can get rid of them. They have killed three chicks this year." She spat into the dirt. "God must have some purpose for the cursed *fourmi rouge*. But I hate the big red ones."

Lily nodded, feeling only a little ashamed that she had assumed her brothers were playing instead of working. Most often when she assumed this, she was right. Augustin was usually figuring out how to avoid work, and Pierre would just trail his older brother around.

"*Non, non*, Rose Eva," Maman said, turning to

swoop up Lily's three-year-old sister. "Stay away from the dye kettle. You could scald yourself!"

"*Brulant!*" Rose Eva said gravely, her little mouth in a straight, serious line.

"Boiling hot!" Maman agreed. "And you could hurt yourself." She kissed Rose Eva's cheek and set her down again, keeping hold of her hand.

"I wonder if the boys followed your father. I will stir a moment, Lily, if you will go look."

Lily nodded and waited until her mother nudged Rose Eva back inside, calling out for Marie to watch her. When Maman took the long handle, she made a shooing motion. "Go quickly. I think they would not dare leave without telling me, but that Augustin is beginning to consider himself a man."

Lily nodded but didn't say anything. Every time she complained to her mother about something Augustin did, Maman would scold him, and that only seemed to make things worse.

Lily started down the path toward the levee, walking as fast as she could. Placing her left foot carefully as she always did, she kept her crooked ankle from turning beneath her weight. She ran in an uneven rhythm that was hers alone.

Going up the steep slant of the levee, Lily turned sideways, taking a big step with her strong leg, then hitching her left foot alongside. Once she was at the top, she stopped and stood still, turning in a slow circle.

The pirogue was still there, and so was the little raft the boys had made earlier in the year. The *bateau* was gone, but that only meant her father was still out gathering moss.

"What do you see?" Maman called.

Lily gestured at her to wait a moment, then shaded her eyes, looking up the bayou. The sun was bright where she stood, but just a little farther south was a stand of live oak trees that cast dappled shadows over the dark water. Farther still, the tupelo gums and palmettos grew thickly along the banks. Every family had cleared enough ground to build a planked dock that jutted out over the warm, slow water.

The bayou was empty as far as Lily could see. Looking north, there was no sign of her brothers, either. The sun shone on 'Nonc Jean's gardens. His place—and those of the rest of the LeGrands—were better kept than almost anyone else's: hardly a shred of palmettos or tupelos growing behind the levees. Their fields went farther back, too. Only at the far end of their long, narrow farms did they permit the natural growth of the swamp.

"Lily!"

She turned to face her mother. "The pirogue is here, and their raft. I don't see them or hear them."

"Pas responsable!" Maman called.

Lily nodded. It was true. Augustin had become irresponsible lately. Lily started back toward the house.

"I will finish here," Maman said as she got closer. "Keep looking for your brothers. They can't be far."

Lily nodded and went around the side of the house, knowing that if Rose Eva or Marie saw her, they would want to tag along. She would be glad when they were both old enough to help more. There were days when she and Maman were too tired to eat in the evenings.

The pigs were in the indigo patch, and she chased them out, relatching the gate they had pushed open. Milk and rice hulls were still in their trough, so they went back into their own pen happily enough, squealing and snorting. Lily glanced at the cage à poulet. The tall, black rooster was crowing from a fence post, his hens scratching at the dark, moist soil beneath. There was no sign of Augustin or Pierre.

Lily crossed the yard and walked around the back of the chicken coop. There were ashes piled six or seven inches deep, heaped into feathery mounds, all along the back wall. So the boys had finished that chore, at least. She could see the big red ants struggling to find their way through the suffocating powder. Straightening, her hands on her hips, Lily squinted to see through the shadows beneath the trees that marked the end of the yard and the beginning of the cornfield. She listened, hoping that her brothers had heard the crows too, and were out there, but she still couldn't hear their voices.

Sighing, Lily walked across the yard, glancing into the cowshed as she passed. Earlier that morning, she had hung the bucket, clean and dry, ready for the evening's milking. The stall was still wet and full of manure. So the boys had not even started their regular chores yet.

Lily made her way, careful not to twist her weak ankle where the ground was muddy. A little farther on, she scuffed her bare feet in the grass to clean them off, then tried to miss the worst places.

Maman always hated it when Lily stained her hem-lines, and now that Lily had begun helping with the weaving and sewing, she understood why.

"Augustin!" Lily shouted as she started down the slope toward the first rice field. There was no answer. Lily walked a little farther, then called her brother's name again. She was a half mile or more from the house, almost to the wild swamp, before she got an answer.

Augustin and Pierre came running when they heard the impatience in her voice. They tumbled over each other in their eagerness to apologize. She knew they were sorry, but it was more than that. They didn't want her to tell Maman that they had been playing.

"I heard crows," she told them, and watched their faces become solemn. "And the cow's stall is filthy."

"That was Pierre's job this morning," Augustin defended himself.

Pierre was shaking his head. "I did it yesterday."

"Go do it now!" Lily interrupted them. "Let Augustin throw stones at the crows. His aim is truer."

Pierre looked insulted. He pulled himself up to

his full height, the very image of eight-year-old dignity. "That is a lie." He looked so stricken, so insulted, that Lily could not help but laugh. Augustin joined her, his mouth twitching at the corners. Pierre allowed his expression to dissolve into a grin.

"Just go, both of you!" Lily said. They shot her grateful looks, knowing now that they would not get into much trouble. Then they ran back toward the house.

Lily followed their footprints, stopping to step over puddles they had leaped, skirting bushes they had burst through. By the time she ducked out of the shade of the live oaks and went back around to the front of the house, her father had arrived home.

"Lily!" he called when he saw her. "Everyone is too busy to come with me. I need your help."

"Of course, Papa," she called back.

He smiled at her. "I just have to deliver the moss to Monsieur Courville, then we will come home. I—"

"Do I have to go?" Lily interrupted, her stomach tightening.

"It will be faster with two of us to paddle," he said.

Lily started to plead, then pressed her lips together.

Her father could not begin to understand why she hated going to the Courville plantation.

Lily had never told him why, and she never intended to. It would only make him start a fight he could not win. She blinked back tears and swallowed hard, turning so Papa could not see her face. "I will wash up," she said over her shoulder. Then she forced herself to start for the house.

Chapter Two

Paul Courville was trying to keep his head down, trying to concentrate on the plate of biscuits and gravy that lay before him on the polished tabletop. His three older brothers were talking, all of them excited and happy this morning. John was going with Father to an auction in New Orleans to buy mules. That meant the twins would be able to get away with anything for a few days—William would lead and Mark would follow along like he always did. Mr. Thomas couldn't control them. He would be busy supervising the planting and the harvest, riding back and forth all day long, shouting orders at the slaves.

"Don't forget to bring me the whetstone," William was saying.

Paul glanced up in time to see John nodding. "I won't

forget. And Mark's gun flints. Do you want anything, Paul?"

"Hair ribbons," William whispered, and John shot him a harsh look.

"I don't need anything," Paul said, meeting John's eyes. Lately John had been telling him that he had to stand up for himself with the twins. But it wasn't that easy.

"Are you sure?" Mark asked, forcing his voice to sound high and squeaky like Paul's. Then he dropped it to a whisper again. "Blue ribbons would set off that jacket."

William laughed approvingly. Paul acted like he hadn't heard. He was praying every night that his voice would change soon and stop squeaking like a girl's every time he opened his mouth. He glanced through the half doors into the parlor where Angeline wielded the feather duster. Mother was having the slaves clean the house thoroughly. She had house-guests coming in five days.

"Father said if he saw a good horse at the sale, he would buy it for me," William said.

Paul glanced at him resentfully. William loved to ride and he was a good horseman, but he already owned a gelding that was sleek and fast. Paul's own horse was an aging mare—calm, gentle, and slow-footed. It wasn't fair. If anyone was going to get another horse, it should be he. But William had the nerve to ask, and that made all the difference with Father.

"You two stay out of trouble while I am gone," John was saying sternly, his brow furrowed in an imitation of Father's. Paul glanced up sharply, still angry over the idea of William getting a new horse. His irritation increased at the tone of his older brother's warning. Had it always been like this? Had John always assumed the twins would have some adventure that could turn dangerous while he was safe at home with Mother? They weren't that much older than he was—only a year and a half.

"And don't cause problems with Mr. Thomas," John added. When the twins didn't answer him, John cleared his throat. "I mean it. You leave the hounds and the fighting cocks alone."

"We only did that once and—" William began.

"And once was enough," John said, interrupting him.

"Are you ready, son?"

Paul was startled by the sound of his father's booming voice.

"Almost," John answered.

Paul watched as Father came into the dining room. His lion's mane of ginger-colored hair was silhouetted against the morning sun streaming through the glass-paned French doors.

Earlier, the doors had been opened wide to catch the coolest morning air. They would be closed until evening. In an hour or so, thick curtains would be drawn against the beginnings of the day's heat. The gauzy mosquito netting would remain neatly gathered aside until midafternoon.

"I would like to make an early start, John," Father said, coming around the table. He turned a chair around, then straddled it, his eyes on his oldest son.

Paul watched William and Mark shift uneasily. Father rarely addressed them, either. All his attention went to John—his heir. He wanted to make sure John knew everything there was to know about running Fair Oaks. What the rest of them did with their futures was of less concern to him as long as they didn't embarrass the family or end up on the wrong side of the law.

John stood, wiped his mouth, then set the white linen napkin on the table. Esther appeared out of nowhere and took his plate and the soiled napkin away. She moved with quick grace and long practice and was gone before Paul's father had noticed her. He rarely noticed any of the house slaves. Managing the domestic staff was his wife's duty.

"We'll be back in three days," Father was saying as he stood up and turned the chair around to push it beneath the table.

"Look out for a good colt, please, Father," William said. "I want to work with one and train it and—"

"I want to do that too," Mark broke in, interrupting his brother. "Terrence Russel was telling me about a new breed of horse his father was—"

"A yearling would be perfect," William said, talking loudly enough to drown out Mark's words.

Paul watched his father's face darken in annoyance. "You're yapping like puppies. I can't understand either one of you."

"My mare is getting old," Paul said in a low voice. His father glanced at him, but didn't respond. Instead, he motioned at John, and together they walked to the wide door that led out onto the veranda.

Shoving back their chairs, the twins got up from the table, Mark flinging his napkin back over his shoulder. It landed on the floor, and Paul picked it up, earning a smile from Esther as she came forward to clear up the mess. Lagging a dozen steps behind, he followed his older brothers outside.

Father led the way past the gardens, glancing over at the sugarhouse, talking to John over his shoulder. Paul could only hear small bits of his father's comments as he made his way between the sweet potato beds and the rows of okra that stood ready to be picked. On the far side of the garden, near the peach trees his grandfather had planted, Paul slowed a little.

The twins went on, following John and Father. As they started up the rise of the levee, Paul slowed again, then stopped, watching the twins hurry to keep up. They all topped the rise and disappeared. Paul could picture Father and John striding along the planked dock, getting into the *bateau*. Toby and Smith would probably be poling the bateau today. Father would want Toby's opinions on any horses he thought about buying.

Paul leaned against one of the peach trees, knowing his mother would scold him for any stains on the cream-white linen of his jacket. This morning, he didn't care. He looked up at the sky, then down at the dark soil beneath his feet. He could hear the sound of the sugar mill. The mules would be walking their eternal circle, the slaves feeding an endless supply of cut cane in between the turning rollers.

This time of year, the plantation was humming with work, but he took no pleasure in the activity anymore. When he had been younger, he had begged Mother to be allowed to watch the planting, the long lines of slaves carefully placing the sections of seed cane into the soil. He had loved running back and forth between the planting going on in the fields that had been fallow the year before and the harvest that took place at the same time.

Then, a year or two ago, his mother had explained to him that the plantation would one day belong to John. Only then had it dawned on him there was little point in learning any more about sugar growing. Mama's face and voice had been soft and sad. She had explained that even though he was the one who liked farming, John was the oldest and that was that. He would inherit everything. It would be up to Paul and the twins to make their lives elsewhere.

"And where that will be, none of us knows," Paul said aloud. He glanced back toward the house. His mother would not rise for another hour or two. And even then, she would not think to ask the slaves where he was for another hour. It would be noon or later before she decided she needed company—and that he needed the civilizing influence of reading aloud or drawing. She was determined to teach him French, too. It was only a matter of time before she found a tutor. She was dedicated to the idea that he would be cultured. She had given up on John and the twins. Every night he prayed she would soon give up on him, too.

"Race?" William shouted, reappearing at the top of the levee.

Mark nodded. "Last one there forfeits his right to any colt Father brings home."

William counted to three, and they were off. They cut across the long slope at an angle, pounding past Paul—barely fifty feet away—without seeing him. Their voices were loud, fading as they got farther away. Paul watched them go, counting slowly to one hundred. Only then did he step away from the peach tree and walk toward the bayou.

By the time Paul ambled to the top of the levee, his father and brother were nearly out of sight, going around the big bend just north of Fair Oaks. Paul envied his brother the boat ride. The bayou was beautiful this time of year with the first cypress leaves turning to red. Most of the spring and summer flowers were long gone, but the birds were thick now and their odd cries and flashing wings were a fair trade.

A movement on the water caught Paul's attention, and he stared into the distance. It was a bateau, wide and flat-bottomed, but it didn't belong to any of the plantations along Bayou Teche, he was sure. Its cargo was piled in loosely, not baled or tied into bundles.

At first, Paul thought it might be a Cajun coming downriver with a load of loose cotton. Then, as the bateau drew closer, he saw he was only half right. It was a Cajun, all right; the man's long, lanky frame was dressed in bright-colored, hand-spun clothing. But the load, in spite of its light color in the morning sun, was not cotton. It was the silvery gray of Spanish moss.

The bateau came on, and Paul stared at it, glancing

past it only once to see that his father and brother had rounded the bend and were out of sight. He slouched into a sitting position, sure that dust on his trousers would be no more trouble than the bark stains on his jacket. His mother would sigh and frown, but that would be all.

When the bateau cleared the last draping branches of the cypress stand, he recognized the man holding the long pole with such skill. It was Monsieur Luc LeGrand. Paul scrambled to his feet, squinting into the sun. Lily was with her father. As usual, she was sitting in the stern of the boat, wielding a paddle.

Paul glanced toward the sugarhouse. Maybe Mark and William wouldn't see Lily and her father. Maybe Monsieur LeGrand wasn't coming to Fair Oaks at all this time. Father had not said anything. But it would be Mr. Thomas who would know.

Paul waved once, but if Lily saw him, she gave no sign. Her father poled the bateau steadily along, then switched to a paddle to cross the deeper water in the center of the bayou. Once he began to pole again, there was little doubt in Paul's mind: Monsieur LeGrand was heading straight for the Fair Oaks dock.

Spinning around, Paul started for the sugarhouse,

prepared to tell his brothers a fib—anything that would make them race back to the house or to the stables, or anywhere they would be preoccupied for the next half hour or so. Running, he cut through the orchard, breathing in the dense, sharp smell of the boiling sugar syrup as he got closer.

Coming around the side of the building, he saw Jedediah, standing with the switch, keeping the mule's pace even as they circled the mill shaft.

"Where are my brothers?" Paul shouted.

Jedediah looked up, and Paul shouted the question again. Jedediah started to shake his head, then his face lit as he looked past Paul. He pointed, and Paul whirled around to face the levee again. The twins were running along the top of it. As he watched, they slowed, laughing. Then William started off again, limping in an exaggerated, grotesque manner, one arm flailing out in a cruel imitation of Lily's labored walk. It was too late. They had seen the bateau.

Chapter Three

At the sound of muffled laughter, Lily glanced back along the levee. Then, lifting her chin and keeping her face expressionless, she pretended she did not see the boys mimicking her awkward walk. Papa did not see them, she was sure. They were clever, those two. They knew Papa would be concentrating just now, angling the flat-bottomed boat toward the planked landing. As Papa eased the bateau forward, Lily allowed herself one more glance backward. The levee was empty now. The boys had run off.

"Climb up and fix the rope, Lily," Papa said.

She nodded, then worked her way around the pile of moss that filled the bateau. Once Papa had the pole braced solidly against the muddy bottom of the bayou, she scrambled up onto the dock. There were iron rings bolted into the planks. She caught the mooring rope when Papa tossed it toward her.

"This won't take long," he said, lifting the pole to slide it onto the dock, muddied end first.

Lily nodded and drew the long line through the mooring ring, then knotted it quickly. Papa was already unloading, standing in the bateau to throw big armloads of the moss onto the landing. As he worked, Lily dragged the moss into a pile, centering it on the landing. She had helped her father many times, and there was little need for talk.

As the pile of moss grew, the load in the bateau shrank until Papa was bent over, raking the last strands together with his fingers. He set the final armload on the planks, then, in one swift motion, sprang from the boat to the landing. "They will make us wait, of course," he said. "Not one of them will act like he has noticed we are here."

Lily had been resisting the urge to scan the top of the levee, but now she did so. The twins were nowhere in sight. Neither was Paul. John would be with his father, wherever that might be. Her father motioned for her to follow, and she did, careful not to drag her left foot. The cypress planks were full of wicked splinters.

Lily slipped once on the levee slope, but did not fall. She followed her father to the top, then paused because he did. From up here she could see the whole of Fair Oaks. The sugarhouse had smoke rising from its chimneys. The springhouse door stood open, and there were two slaves carrying casks inside. A cart pulled by two mules was making its slow, ponderous way toward the sugar mill from a field beyond the big house. And to the south, Lily could see hoes flashing in the early sun. Next year's seed cane was being planted. She could hear the weary cadence of a hymn. Someone was singing to pass the dreary hours of work.

"I'll go find someone," Papa said. "Mr. Thomas has to be around somewhere."

"Yes, Papa," Lily said.

"You stay close to the bateau. Anyone who comes along might take an armload or two of the moss, and the weight could come up short."

Lily nodded, glad he didn't want her to traipse across the plantation with him. If she was lucky, the twins would forget she was around. She tried to spot them and couldn't. Maybe they were already busy at something else.

"I won't be long," Papa said as he started down the slope of the levee. Lily watched him head across the orchard, reaching out to pluck a peach as he went. Her mouth watered. Maybe he would bring one back for her when he came, if Mr. Thomas didn't insist on walking with him. Lily sighed. The straight-backed old Englishman would probably keep an eye on Papa from the moment he realized he was there. Although he was never rude, it was obvious Mr. Thomas had little use for Cajuns. And he would certainly never consider throwing in a few peaches for *langiappe* to sweeten the deal for the moss.

Lily went down the slope slowly, careful not to trust her left foot to carry her weight for more than a second or two. The Fair Oaks levee was steeper than the one at home, and a lot higher.

Lily walked out onto the landing, looking in both directions as she went. There was a steamer far to the north, its plume of white smoke drifting back along the bayou. They had passed it on their way south-ward, nearly an hour before. It must have stopped to take on firewood.

Lily heard a hissing sound and stepped back, startled, her reaction swifter than her thought. As she staggered to one side, catching her balance, she stared at the edge of the pile of moss, her eyes searching for movement. But of course there was no snake on the landing. How could there be? If there had been a snake in the moss they had gathered, they would have seen it long before this.

Lily stared down at the planks, then looked up, puzzled. What had she heard? She stood for a long moment, listening intently. She shook her head. "Papa will be back in a few minutes," she said aloud to reassure herself. "You are just nervous here."

Still uneasy, Lily picked up the bateau pole and lowered the muddy end into the water to wash it clean. Then she jabbed at the moss pile, standing well back, every muscle in her body tense and ready. But there was no snake. Glancing behind herself, hoping no one had seen her poking at the moss like a fool, Lily laid the pole down. She sat cross-legged on the landing, using a little moss to cushion the hard planks.

The hissing sound came once more, and Lily leaped up, her heart pounding. She had not imagined it, and it had been close, very close. She lurched forward and picked up the pole again, facing the moss pile. She shoved the pole into the moss over and over, listening again for the dreaded sound. It did not come.

Lily dropped the pole, letting it clatter against the wood landing. She wiped the sweat from her forehead and squinted into the sun. It was getting hot. By midday it would be worse. She sank back down onto the planks and let out a long, slow breath. It was only then she noticed that the mooring line had been untied.

Heaving herself to her feet once more, Lily whirled around to look southward. There, bobbing on the almost nonexistent current, was the bateau. It was only a little ways from the dock, but it was well beyond the reach of the pole. Lily stood still for a few seconds, thinking furiously.

She didn't have to wonder who had untied the mooring rope; she knew: Mark and William had made the hissing sounds from beneath the docks. It had fooled her long enough for them to run away. They might still be watching from a distance, she knew, but the clear slope of the levee was empty as far as she could see in both directions. They couldn't be too close.

Lily slipped her dress over her head and stood in her chemise, trembling with anger. Then, knowing there was nothing else she could do, she went to the edge of the landing and dove into the brown water.

In the water, Lily's lame foot did not slow her down. If anything, its odd, turned-in angle helped her swim. As furious and upset as she was, the water still gave her what it always did: a feeling of grace and weightlessness that nothing else ever did.

Lily swam fast and, in seconds, had reached the bateau. Hooking one arm over the low stern, she towed it back toward the landing, her legs moving in powerful circles like a frog's. She was almost there when she heard the clattering of boots on the dock and whirled around in the water, craning her neck to see.

William and Mark were running, leaping from the dock back to the levee, laughing. Lily beat her fist against the side of the bateau, helpless to do anything but watch them disappear. Hot tears of fury stinging her eyes, she towed the bateau close enough to retie the mooring rope.

Shivering in spite of the hot sun, knowing the twins were watching, Lily swam to the toe of the levee and waded out. She ran as fast as she could, acutely aware of her lurching gate. She rounded the end of the dock, jumping back up onto the planks, losing her balance but regaining it before she fell.

What she saw made her bite her own lip to keep from screaming. They had scattered the moss from one end of the dock to the other. And her dress was nowhere to be seen. Numb with fury, Lily began gathering the moss.

"I will get them for this," she whispered over and over like an angry prayer. "I will."

She managed to gather most of the moss. At least they had not thrown it into the water. She was afraid of what Papa would say, what he might do. Monsieur Courville was a rich and powerful man. Papa would either have to remain silent, as she had always done, or risk making a dangerous enemy.

Lily shuddered, thinking about what Maman would say when she saw that a month's worth of weaving and sewing had been lost. Lily felt tears stinging at her eyes again and she crossed her arms, feeling helpless. She couldn't chase the boys in her chemise. Papa would be ashamed of her when he came back and found her standing here in her underclothes.

Out of the corner of her eye, Lily saw someone on top of the levee. She turned away, blushing and trying not to cry, glancing back over her shoulder. But it wasn't the twins, and it wasn't her father.

Paul Courville stood uncertainly at the top of the levee. "Are you all right?" he called.

She nodded, then shook her head. "Your brothers—"

"They told me," he said in a low, apologetic voice. "They're proud of themselves, I guess."

Lily turned to face him. "Where did they put my dress?"

She watched him shrug, then frown. "They didn't tell me, but I saw them climbing one of the old oaks."

Lily shivered again. "Maybe they hid it?"

Paul nodded. "Maybe."

"Where's my father? If he sees me like this—"

Paul straightened up and tugged at his sleeve, shrugging out of his linen jacket. Without a word, he put it around her shoulders and looked into her face. "I'll find your dress if I can."

Lily wanted to thank him. She wanted to tell him she was grateful he never joined in with the teasing, never helped his brothers make fun of her. But he was already starting back up the levee, his face set and grim.

Chapter Four

Paul walked fast until he knew Lily couldn't see him. Then he stopped, trying to figure out where his brothers would be hiding. He walked deliberately forward, listening intently for muffled laughter. When none came, he veered slightly, passing the shadowy copse of pecan trees in the paddock above the stable.

Whistling, acting as though he did not have a care in the world, Paul pretended to stroll aimlessly across the garden. Only then did he turn and head for the stand of old oaks he had seen his brothers climbing. If they had hidden the dress, he knew where it was. There was a squirrel hole up about twenty feet in one of the broad-trunked oaks. The twins had been using it for a hiding place as long as he could remember.

Glancing around, Paul approached the tree cautiously.

Then, when he was sure no one was close enough to see what he was doing, he peeled off his vest. Leaving it draped over a low branch, he took off his shoes, then began to climb. Halfway up, he heard a shout.

"What in blazes do you think you're doing!"

Paul looked down, his heart pounding. William was at the base of the tree, his hands on his hips.

"I wanted to spot the midday steamboat heading south," Paul said, trying to keep his voice steady.

His brothers would not actually beat him up. They would get in too much trouble for that. But they could make his life miserable with their tricks.

"Come down now," William said slowly. He glanced over his shoulder, and Paul knew Mark was somewhere nearby.

"I want to spot the—" Paul began.

"I said come down," William repeated.

Paul sighed. He started to shift his weight, preparing to start down, but something stopped him. It was wrong for his brothers to torment Lily. He had talked to her a number of times and he had never heard her utter an ill-spirited word about anyone— not even the twins.

"The joke has gone far enough," Paul said.

Below him, William shook his head. "That's not up to you."

Paul pulled in another deep breath. "She has enough trouble in her life without you two—"

"Those swamp Cajuns don't deserve your pity, Paul," his brother interrupted. "The Cajun girls aren't delicate like the girls you know. She probably thinks it's funny."

"She doesn't think anything like that," Paul said, and he found himself getting angry. It felt good. It made him less afraid. Ignoring his brother's shouts, he made his way upward, reaching into the rough-barked cavity in the trunk of the tree. Just as he had thought, Lily's dress was inside. He pulled it out and put it over his shoulders like a shawl to free his hands for the climb down.

"Put it back!" It was Mark's voice, a little less deep and rough than William's. Paul looked down and saw them standing side by side now.

"I'm going to take it back to her," Paul said. He looked out toward the levee. From his perch in the tree, he could just see the dock. Lily was alone, standing close to the pile of moss. Her father was probably still dickering over a price with Mr. Thomas.

"Maybe you would like to strike a bargain?" William said, a sneer in his voice.

Paul looked down. They were only ten or so feet below him now. Mark had Paul's vest and was holding it lightly between his two fingers, swinging it back and forth like a pendulum. "He already gave that girl his jacket," Paul heard Mark whisper to William.

"You did what?" William demanded, looking up through the branches.

"She was in her chemise and petticoat," Paul answered. "I couldn't just leave her standing there shivering. Her father—"

"Her father doesn't care about proper attire, Paul," William interrupted. "They live in those little mud-plaster cabins with ten of them in three rooms. They're too lazy to make proper houses."

Paul stared down into his brother's face. William refused to do most of the chores Papa gave him. And Mark wasn't much better. For either one of them to call someone else lazy was so funny, Paul had to concentrate not to laugh as he came farther down the tree.

"Maybe we will just throw the dress in the kennel and let the dogs tear it up," William threatened. Mark nodded hesitantly.

Paul jumped the last few feet to the ground. "Get out of my way."

"We want the dress. You want your vest," William said. "Let's just trade and get it over with."

Paul shook his head. "Do what you want with it," he said, moving a little to one side, glancing down at his shoes, hidden by the tall grass. William followed his glance and leaped to grab them. He danced back, holding the shoes high above his head.

"Do what you want with those, too," Paul said, backing up one step, then another, the warm dirt gritty beneath his bare feet.

"We'll throw them in the bayou and tell Mother you did it," William insisted.

Paul stared at his brothers. For the first time in his life, they didn't look older, bigger, and intimidating. They just looked foolish. "I'll tell Mother the truth," he said quietly.

William laughed, and Mark joined in, but there was a strained edge to their voices. Paul took one more step backward, tying Lily's dress loosely around his shoulders like an old woman ties her shawl. He could see the confusion in William's eyes, and he smiled a little, looking straight at his brother. Then, without warning, he took off running, dodging just enough to one side to get around them.

"You get back here!" he heard William shout, then there was only the sound of footsteps behind him.

Paul ran like he had never run before. Freed from his coat and shoes, he felt like he could fly over the ground. The dirt was soft in the orchard, and he sprinted, hearing his brothers' angry shouts behind him.

Then, about halfway across the wide field, they stopped shouting. He wasn't sure why, but he could guess. Maybe they had seen Mr. Thomas or Lily's father—or maybe it had just occurred to them that if they yelled loud enough, someone might notice. Either way, Paul was grateful for the silence and he ran on, ignoring his tender feet.

At the top of the levee he slowed just enough to glance backward before starting down the slope that led to the landing. William was holding up his shoes, and Mark had his vest. But they had stopped, half concealed by the last row of pecan trees.

Turning to face Lily, Paul saw she had sat down and had pulled some of the moss over herself. As he approached he loosened the knot in her dress. She jumped to her feet and ran toward him in her peculiar lurching gait, reaching out to take it.

Lily clutched the dress, smiling at him. She turned her back and slipped out of his jacket and slid her dress on over her head. Then she faced him and shyly handed his jacket to him. "Your handkerchief is in the pocket. It's a little damp. I used it to wipe my face."

Paul nodded and put on his jacket, then stood awkwardly, still breathing hard from his run. Her dress had gotten a little muddy. Still, she was beaming at him as though he had given her a wonderful present.

"I'm sorry about them," he said, gesturing.

"My brother Augustin put a snake in my bed once." She said it almost without inflection, like someone remarking on the weather.

"What did you do?" Paul asked.

Her smile became a grin. "I put a bucketful of crayfish in his."

Paul was so glad she wasn't angry with him that he laughed aloud. "Did you get in trouble?"

"Yes." She smoothed the front of her dress. The heavy, homespun cotton was full of wrinkles. "It was worth it."

There was something about the lilting way she

spoke and her impish smile that made him laugh again. She laughed with him.

"Lily!"

The sound of her father's voice made Paul whirl around. The tall, dark-haired man was glaring at him.

"I nearly fell into the water, Papa," Lily said quickly. "Paul saw me and ran to help."

Paul saw the protective anger in the tall man's eyes as he reached out to touch his daughter's cheek. Then he thanked Paul brusquely and hurried her off, steadying her as she climbed down into the bateau. Paul stood watching as Lily's father poled the flat-bottomed boat back up the bayou. If he found out the truth, he would be furious that Lily had been unchaperoned—and improperly dressed— talking with a boy.

Finally, Lily turned and waved. Paul waved back.

"Oh, fair damsel, how I love thee!" It was William's voice, high and quavery.

Paul did not bother to turn. Even when he heard the first small splash, he refused to give his brothers the satisfaction of seeing him upset. He would tell the truth about his shoes, and about Lily's dress, he decided.

"If you apologize to us," William said in a low voice, "I will give you your vest back."

"But you have to be very sincere," Mark added.

Paul turned around slowly, glaring at them. They looked ridiculous. Their hair was unruly, their own clothes dirty from climbing the oak. And they were standing side by side, a pair of bookend bullies.

"I told you before, do whatever you like," Paul said flatly. Then he started up the levee and headed toward the house without looking back.

Chapter Five

The next day, Paul stayed close to the house, going to the sugarhouse only once when Mother sent him to get Mr. Thomas. William and Mark kept to themselves, and Paul was glad. Mother was upset about his missing shoes and vest, but she believed him. She was stern with William and Mark, promising them that Father would have more to say about the matter once he got home.

The day after that, Paul began to think his brothers were going to let well enough alone. They were quiet at breakfast, then disappeared until almost dinnertime.

Paul spent a dreary, hot afternoon listening to his mother read poetry. After her second go-through of Poe's "Annabel Lee," Paul offered to help her wind spools of cotton yarn, just to make her stop. The heavy heat that had let up for a week or so came back with a vengeance, making the September afternoon feel more like high summer.

When it finally cooled off a little, and Mother was sequestered in her chambers for the evening, William reappeared. "Your lady friend is down at the landing," he said as he came through the mosquito cloth that hung over the door.

Paul looked up. "What?"

"The Cajun girl," William said. "She's down there with her father."

Paul stood up, hesitating. "She is? Why are they here so late in the day?"

William shrugged. "Another load of moss. I guess Mr. Thomas needed more."

Paul studied his brother. "And you just thought you'd be nice enough to tell me?"

William stared at the floor. "We felt bad about that last time."

"Thanks," Paul said sarcastically.

William made a mock bow. "She said to ask you to hurry."

"I will do just that," Paul answered, to make William

go away. He stood silently, watching his brother turn and walk back outside. He was not about to fall for one of the twins' tricks. He waited for William to come back in, to keep trying to get him outside.

Paul could hear the captain's clock in the parlor. The house was quiet, the afternoon heat heavy and still. He heard William shouting something, then an answer from Mr. Thomas. Maybe Lily and her father really were down at the dock. He didn't want Lily to think he didn't care about seeing her.

"If Mother asks where I have gone," Paul called to Esther, "please tell her I'll be back in before dark." He waited just long enough to hear Esther's answer, then he hurried outside.

Paul crossed the orchard and climbed the levee, sweating in the humid heat. At the top, he stopped. There was no one at the landing. He looked north along the bayou, then southward. Clenching his fists, he waited for the mocking laughter of his brothers.

For nearly a half minute, there was no sound. Paul turned. They were standing behind him on the levee slope. Together, they came forward, walking fast. Mark took his left arm, William took his right, and they forced him to march between them all the way down to the landing.

Without speaking, they pushed and pulled him along, wrestling him into one of the bateaus Father used for supply trips to Lafayette. When Paul shouted for help, William clapped a hand across his mouth and leaned forward, speaking only a few inches from his face. "Just sit still, for heaven's sake, and stop acting like a scared baby."

Paul clenched his jaw and stared at William as Mark untied the mooring rope. "Where are you taking me?"

William shrugged. "We just thought you might want to see your lady friend—"

"She is not my lady friend," Paul began. "And she isn't here. What are you—"

William held up one hand. "Hush up."

"When Father gets home, we are going to be in trouble, thanks to you," Mark said, dragging the long pole forward. Then he plunged it nearly straight downward to the muddy bottom, pushing hard so that the bateau lurched away from the landing.

Paul squinted in the bright sun, measuring the distance between where he sat and the shoreline.

"Don't even think about it," William said. "You know I can outswim you."

Paul slumped on the wooden bench. This was the story of his whole life. His brothers were all bigger and stronger, and as much as he hated admitting it, they were smarter. He should have refused to come outside. He should have known they would be planning some get-even trick.

"How long do you think it will take for him to learn?" William asked Mark.

Mark shrugged. "An hour? Maybe two?"

"Two hours of what?" Paul demanded.

Mark was poling awkwardly and didn't answer. William scowled at him. When they refused to break their silence, there was nothing Paul could do but glare at them angrily.

After a long time, William took a turn with the pole. Paul kept waiting for them to make him do the work, but they pretended not to notice him at all. The sunshine fell heavily on Paul's scalp and shoulders, and sweat coated his brow.

Finally, William maneuvered the bateau into a backwater, slowing down.

"Where are you going?" Paul repeated.

Neither of his brothers answered. Instead, Mark took the pole and moved the bateau silently past a big cypress, its roots jutting up like smooth-barked knees all around it. He was not that good at handling the bateau in the narrower channels, but he kept going.

"You're going to get us all lost back in here," Paul said angrily.

William pretended to sob, covering his face with his hands. Then he looked up, grinning. "Boo-hoo, Paul is getting lost."

Sorry he hadn't tried to swim when he'd had the chance, Paul scowled at his brother. "Father forbade us to get out of sight of the Teche." He looked backward. The curtains of Spanish moss that hung from the cypress trees made it impossible to see the wider expanse of dark water behind them.

"Look out!" William shouted.

Paul wrenched around in time to see a low-hanging limb coming straight at him. He ducked, and the bateau skimmed beneath it. The rough bark chafed Paul's shoulder, and he heard William curse. A second later they were clear of the tree, and Mark was sitting up again, rubbing the back of his right hand.

"Watch where you're going!" William said angrily. He stood up and tried to wrest the pole away from Mark. Paul scrambled back out of the way, nearly falling over the stern. He caught himself at the last second.

"If you think you can do it better, go ahead," Mark was shouting.

"Let's just go home now," Paul said, straightening up.

Without answering, William reached out and jerked the long, slender pole away from Mark. Then he stood up, motioning sharply. The bateau, with its wide, flat bottom, barely tilted as the twins exchanged places. Mark sat down on the front bench.

"You've had your joke," Paul said. "Now let's go back."

"Not yet, Paul," William said.

Paul sighed. The day he was old enough, he promised himself, he would find work on a sailing ship and go far, far away from his brothers. The way he felt right now, he could easily imagine never wanting to come back.

William was better at poling the bateau than Mark was. He kept them moving, struggling to follow the curve of whatever narrow waterway they had turned into.

Paul kept glancing back, trying to memorize landmarks, but it was impossible. The swamp was a tangle of vines and lacy Spanish moss. Tufted grass grew out of the shallows, and the waterways twisted across the earth. William followed first one, then another, poling the bateau along in grim silence.

"I think this is far enough," Mark said as they slid past another of the countless cypress trees.

"You're as big a baby as he is, then," William said, sneering.

Paul glanced back again, and the endless swamp seemed to stretch out from the bateau in every direction. The gloom beneath the trees was broken up by splintered shafts of sunlight and ink-dark shadows. Paul blinked. Was it getting dusky? There was no sign of their passing—not a ripple, not a mark. How could they ever retrace the way they had come?

Chapter Six

The sun was almost up. In the light of the lantern, Lily cut a thin, perfect line down the belly of the dead muskrat. Then she slit the skin in circles just above all four paws and around the neck. Some people left the heads on, but Papa did not. Too many of the furs were spoiled that way.

Lily slid the skin off the muskrat, using the edge of the knife to cut it away from the flesh and muscle that lay below. She was careful not to pierce the gland beneath the tail—the musk oil had an odor so strong, it could make a person's eyes water, and it would ruin the pelt.

She added the skin to the pile, fur down, and scattered salt over it. She began to hum. She didn't mind skinning muskrats. Since they never ate the meat, she didn't have to gut them—her least favorite part of any butchering job.

When Lily was finished, she buried the carcasses at the edge of the garden, then carried the skins inside. Maman looked up as she opened the door. When she saw the pile of skins, she smiled, then frowned. "This is not work fit for a girl your age," she said, shaking her head.

Lily smiled. She didn't want to upset her mother, but the truth was, she liked skinning and dressing meat better than kitchen work. She could smell the warm scent of the stock Maman was boiling and was glad she had not been the one to roast the fish bones and stir the crayfish shells. "I don't mind skinning, Maman, and the boys will be old enough soon."

"Not soon enough for me," Maman said, stirring the stock. "I don't know how you will ever find a husband unless he is too lazy to do his own work and wants you to do it for him." She reached out to touch Lily's hair. "Such a pretty color. You are a lovely girl. If your sisters are as pretty, we will have more fights among the young men at every *fais do-do*."

Lily laughed. "Maman, I cannot even dance. Why would I want to go at all?"

Maman stood straight and looked at Lily, feigning sternness. "My sisters and I are all born dancers. You run in spite of your weak ankle; you do everything. You are growing up, Lily. You will dance."

Lily smiled. In Maman's little round mirror, even she could see that her face was changing. Sometimes now she looked into the swamp water if she could find a still place with enough sunlight coming through the trees to make a reflection.

"Wash up, pretty girl," Maman said. "And begin the roux for supper. I want to make a gumbo with the fish your father brought home last night."

Lily nodded. "Where are Marie and Rose Eva?"

Maman gestured toward the back of the house. "Asleep. Waiting for the heat to pass."

Wishing she could nap away the afternoon with her little sisters, Lily headed for the *tablette*. Using water from the oak bucket and the strong French soap her mother favored, she scrubbed her arms up to her elbows. Drying herself on a clean cotton cloth, she wrinkled her nose at the faint smell of musk that clung to her skin.

Lily got down the flour jar and the coffee tin her mother used to catch fat. Spooning fat into a flat skillet, she slid it into the ashes at the edge of the hearth. Once the fat had melted and begun to sizzle just a little, she sprinkled flour into it, moving the skillet farther from the heat.

Stirring constantly, Lily watched her brothers as they ran in and out of the kitchen, laughing and playing. Maman was chopping onion and garlic into fine pieces. Then she gutted and washed the fish. Lily kept stirring. There was no point in trying to hurry a roux. That would only ruin it and force her to start over.

Lily patiently browned the flour until it was as smooth as silk and beginning to thicken. She kept stirring, wiping her damp brow as she worked. Slowly the flour began to darken, and she pulled the heavy skillet a little ways out of the ashes and continued stirring as the flour cooked. When it was finally the color of dark chocolate, she looked up to find her mother waiting.

"Ready?"

"Yes," Lily answered her mother.

Maman crossed the kitchen with a bowl. She dumped the chopped onion and garlic into the roux. Lily settled the tin lid onto the skillet and shifted its position slightly, pushing it back over the coals.

"Give it an hour or so," her mother said. "You can go see to the animals while I make corn bread."

Lily nodded. But she went out onto the gallerie first, and walked up the gentle slope to the edge of the bayou. Listening to the hum of the water flies and mosquitoes, she followed the short path onto the rough cypress planks of their landing. Papa had taken the bateau, but her pirogue was moored, floating peacefully on the almost motionless water.

Bayou LeGrand was far less wide than Bayou Teche, and it wasn't even a tenth as long. The *petit habitants* she could see were all built of weathered wood, most with *bousillage* chimneys, the mud baked dark and smooth. She knew every person in every house—many of them were her cousins.

The cry of a heron overhead shattered Lily's thoughts. She glanced up at the sky. It was close to noon, now. She longed to get in her pirogue, to paddle into the silent swamp. She loved all the winding channels and the dense hummocks of grass stitched together with fallen logs and endless vines like God's own quilt.

Her grandfather had made her pirogue and had

used it himself for many years. When he lay close to dying, he had given it to her. The boys had gotten his traps and his fishnets. Her father used the boat often, but he always asked her for permission first.

With one more wistful glance at the pirogue, Lily smoothed her apron front and sighed. Then she turned and started back toward the house.

"Lily!"

It was Augustin, standing in the side yard by the indigo patch. His face was flushed with heat, and she could see, as she approached him, that he was excited about something. He reached inside his shirt and drew out a slender green snake.

"What a beauty," Lily said.

Augustin grinned. "Pierre caught it. He's waiting for me up above the cotton field." He lifted the snake high, letting the length of its body slide across his arm. "Maman says I have to put it back in its tree. It is just a baby."

Lily nodded and glanced toward the house. Maman hated snakes. Not only the ones that could kill with a single, swift strike, but even those that would not hurt her.

Augustin let the snake crawl over his shoulder,

then reached back gently to get hold of it again. "This is the smallest one I have seen all summer. Remember the one in the hog pen?"

"It was as long as Papa is tall, I think," Lily said.

Augustin nodded. "At least that."

Lily stroked the cool, smooth scales of the snake. Its tongue flicked over her fingers. "Put it into thick leaves so the hawks don't get it."

Augustin nodded and guided the snake back inside his shirt. "I will. And when we come back, Pierre and I will water and feed the cows."

Lily watched her brother walk away, then turned toward the hog pen. The wallow needed filling soon. The weather had been hot, and the pigs lay in the cool mud constantly.

Lily got the cypress bucket from its hook on the back gallerie. She unwound the rope from around it and used it to lower the bucket into the cistern. She tugged sharply to one side to make the bucket sink. When it was full, she hauled it up and carried it to the pen.

Lily made eleven trips, holding the bucket out from her side to keep her uneven stride from sloshing the water. She poured out each bucketful carefully, filling the muddy hollow. The pigs moved to the rear fence and stood watching her trudge back and forth. When the wallow was finally full, she wrapped the rope back around the bucket and hung it up. A musical whistle from the other side of the house made her smile. Papa was home!

Lily ran through the side yard and up the path toward the landing. Papa was coming toward her, carrying a cotton sack that swung heavily back and forth. "Oysters," he said. "From your *Tante* Marie."

"Maman is making gumbo from the fish," Lily told him. "I made the roux."

He smiled and touched her cheek. "I have other news," he said. "Come inside and I will tell you and Maman at the same time."

Lily followed him inside, curious and uneasy. Usually when Papa made them gather to hear news, it was bad. He hated telling bad things over and over.

Maman met them at the door, flinging it open. The girls were up, playing a game of dolls on the floor. Lily watched her father pick Marie up to kiss her, then Rose Eva. "Where are the boys?"

"Back above the cotton," Lily said. "Pierre caught a green snake, and Augustin went to turn it loose."

Papa nodded gravely. "Well, it is you who will care the most, Lily."

She stared at him, waiting.

"It's the Courville boys. The twins and the younger one—Paul, the one you say is kind. They are all three lost in the swamp. No one has seen them since yesterday."

"What were they doing in the swamp?" Lily asked.

Papa shook his head. "No one seems to know that. Jedediah says people saw the twin brothers fighting the other one."

"Fighting with Paul?"

Papa nodded. "And winning. They pulled him down to the landing and put him in the bateau."

Lily stared at her father, confused. "Why would they do that?"

Papa shrugged. "How could I know this?"

"Is someone looking for them, Papa?" Lily asked.

He shrugged again. "Some of their slaves were sent out, but I can't imagine that they would risk their lives for those boys."

Lily nodded, understanding him. William and Mark were arrogant and mean. "Poor Paul," she said aloud. "Did Jedediah say any more?"

Papa shook his head. "He has to be careful, you know that."

Lily nodded, understanding that Papa had not pressed Jedediah to say more.

"Mr. Thomas refused my help," Papa said abruptly. He shook his head. "Foolish Englishman. Has to prove he can handle this without Cajun help."

"Prove it to—" Maman began.

"To Monsieur Courville," Papa interrupted.

Lily heard them as they went on talking, agreeing that Mr. Thomas wanted to be the only hero in his employer's eyes—and that his pride could easily cost the boys their lives.

Lily's thoughts and feelings tangled around each other. She knew only one thing for certain: Every minute Paul spent in the swamp, he was in danger, terrible danger.

Chapter Seven

Paul had been awake all night, sitting miserably astride a tree limb. His face and hands were splotched and swollen. The mosquitoes had whined around him in a cloud from sunset to sunrise.

His legs ached and his back spasmed, but he didn't want to climb down from his tree. The night had seemed a thousand hours long. Now, in the morning sun, he could finally see that some of the shadowy shapes that had terrified him in the moonlight were only fallen trees. But he could still hear the small, rustling sounds in the grass that reminded him one snakebite could be the end of him forever.

It still amazed him that William and Mark had left him here, choosing the little island because it had a tree he could climb. They had laughed at him when he had asked them to stop joking. William had laughed even harder when Paul had begun to realize they meant it—they were going to leave him alone in the swamp.

No amount of begging had swayed them. And when he had tried to climb on the back of the bateau, Mark had pushed him away while William poled them forward. Paul was ashamed that he had stood, crying and shouting, as they had glided away over the dark water. William must have had an even better laugh later, remembering it.

Paul looked down toward the ground. He was going to have to climb down soon. The pain in his legs and back was more than he could stand. He didn't want to move at all. At least in the tree he knew he was safe from some of the worst dangers of the swamp. He envied the animals that lived here, going about their business without the fear that tightened his stomach every time he heard a strange birdcall or some other sound he couldn't identify.

In the still channel that surrounded his tiny island, Paul could see five or six ducks swimming in lazy circles, diving now and then only to bob back up, shaking water from their backs.

A rustle in the grass below him made Paul wrench

around, trying to see. At first he couldn't spot what was making the noise. But after a moment, he picked out the dull green scales of an alligator from the shifting patterns of dappled sunlight on tall grass.

Paul sat very still. As he stared, the 'gator moved forward very slowly, sliding into the swamp inch by inch. Then, because he was looking straight down at the water, Paul could see the animal swimming under the surface. It went deep enough to prevent any rippling, its tail undulating, propelling it forward.

The ducks swam on, unsuspecting, and as the alligator got closer, Paul held his breath. Suddenly, with more speed than Paul would have believed possible, the alligator rose to the surface, its jaw opening wide, showing its pink gums and tongue and its rows of knifelike teeth.

The duck nearest the 'gator saw the danger coming from below and slashed at the water with its wings, frantic, desperately trying to fly. It couldn't. Mired by the weight of the water, the duck could only thrash backward. The alligator snapped, its jaws shutting with a terrible sound. The duck was pulled beneath the surface.

Paul could see it struggling, one wing pinned in

the 'gator's mouth, the other flailing in the water, its motion slowing each second, until, drowning, it was still.

Lily spent the rest of the afternoon in a fog of confusion and unease. Her father acted as though nothing unusual were happening. Lily knew why. Papa often ignored things he could not help or fix. It was his way. But he had no idea how Paul had helped her. She had never told him the whole story.

It took her several hours to work up her courage. She was afraid of how he might react, but she could not stop imagining Paul lost somewhere in the bayou, scared or hurt, or worse.

Papa was chopping hearth wood when Lily finally managed to get off by herself. She approached him slowly. After a moment, he looked up and saw her watching him. "Your Maman does not need help?"

"The boys are sweeping the front gallerie now."

Papa spat. "That is girl's work."

"I skinned this morning. It was a trade."

Papa grinned. "Fair enough. And I know which you like better." He reached out to tug gently at her hair. "Where is your bonnet?"

She smiled at him, knowing he was only teasing. It was Maman who was serious about wanting her to cover her hair and keep her skin as fair as possible. "Papa, I have to talk to you about something."

His face became grave. "Something about those boys, isn't it?"

"Yes," Lily told him. Then, before he could say anything else, she told him the truth about her rumpled dress—and his face darkened as she spoke. "And they ran and hid it and—" she went on.

"How dare they do something like that?" he interrupted.

Lily hung her head. "They have always mocked me, Papa." She told him about William's lurching parody of her walk.

"Then they deserve whatever happens to them," Papa said in a low angry voice.

"But not Paul," she told him, and explained how the youngest Courville boy was different from his brothers. She watched Papa's face carefully, but it did not soften.

"Mr. Thomas treats me like a beggar whenever I sell him moss or fish. Courville himself never deigns to speak with me at all. Let them hire whatever help they need. I am glad Thomas did not accept my offer."

"But they will never find them," Lily said. "You know they won't!"

"Perhaps not," Papa said. "But even your Maman, gentle soul that she is, saw no reason to help this family. Would they ever help us in time of need? You know they would not."

"Paul helped me. And he has done it before."

Papa shook his head. "I am sorry, Lily."

She clenched her fists and looked at him, tears welling up in her eyes. "Please, Papa."

He shook his head. "I cannot. I spoke with my brother and your mother's father this morning. No one will help. The Courvilles are reaping what they have sown. It has been decided."

Lily stood still a moment longer, just staring into her father's face. He meant it, she knew. He reached out to tug her hair again, but she stepped backward. Her thoughts were reeling in circles. Paul had always tried to make his brothers leave her alone. He was her only friend outside Bayou LeGrand.

"Lily?"

Maman was standing at the back door. "Will you help me for a moment, Lily?"

"Forget about the Courvilles," Papa said. "They will find their own boys. They are nothing to you or to this family, Lily. Not even Paul would help if your brothers were lost."

Lily pressed her lips together. It would do no good to tell him he was wrong. And she knew he was. If she asked Paul for help, he would give it to her. He would. He had risked angering his brothers to save her from embarrassment. What might he have done to save her life?

"I just need you to get the seed out of that last bag of cotton," Maman said. "I will set up the small wheel tomorrow, and we can begin spinning thread."

Lily nodded and followed Maman back inside. She did not turn to look at her father as she closed the door behind herself. After a moment she heard the steady sound of his woodchopping resume.

"Non, non, you two stay out of that," Maman was saying.

Lily turned, but her eyes took a moment to adjust to the dim interior. Rose Eva and Marie were sitting next to a basket filled with scraps of worn cloth, playing at quilt making. Marie had dragged a bigger basket—the one Maman kept filled with her own scraps, pieces of sound cloth she meant to quilt together herself. Maman pushed the big basket against the wall.

"Don't lose the needles," she reminded the girls. Rose Eva held hers up for Maman to see. Her little face was bright with pleasure at being included in the game at all. She was only three and had just recently been trusted with a needle.

Maman sat at the big loom and began slowly, as she always did, careful not to draw the first few passes of the shuttle more tightly than the last few had been drawn. Maman's cloth was remarkably flat and even.

Lily settled herself on the floor with the cotton basket. She began picking seeds, glancing up at Maman every few seconds. "I think Papa should help the Courvilles look for—"

"Are you still worrying over their troubles?" Maman asked. Her voice was gentle and astonished. "Do you think they would spend one second worrying about you?"

Lily nodded, but Maman had turned and was hurrying toward Rose Eva. "Not like that, little one," she scolded quietly. "Hold it just so."

Lily waited until her mother was back at the

loom, then spoke up again. "I told Papa about something that happened—"

Her words were cut short when Rose Eva squealed,
then burst into tears. "Oh, Rose Eva!" Maman exclaimed,
jumping up from her loom again.

Lily could see the drop of blood on her littlest
sister's thumb. With Maman's arms around her, Rose
Eva stopped crying after a moment and steadied
herself, sniffing loudly every few seconds. Maman
showed her once more how to make the simplest
stitch, then walked away once she was happily sewing her play quilt again.

Lily watched her mother, waiting for a quiet
moment to continue their talk. But after a few minutes, the boys burst in the front door, bringing with
them a clatter of broomsticks and rustling palmetto
leaves. They stood the brooms against the wall in
the kitchen, then circled Rose Eva and Marie, reaching into the scrap basket while the girls giggled and
slapped at their hands.

"I need to have someone gather the eggs," Maman
said into the clamor.

"I will!" Pierre shouted, and started for the egg
basket.

Augustin chased him. Because he was taller, he grabbed the basket first, swooshing it past his brother. They went out the back door, still running. Lily saw her father look up from his chopping and grin as the boys raced past him. Lily blinked at the sudden slanting light of the late afternoon sun that poured in the open door.

Sighing, Maman crossed the room to close the door. She ladled a glass of water from the kitchen bucket and drank it down, wiping at her mouth with the back of her hand. "I will be glad when winter comes."

Lily said nothing. She had no idea what to say. She didn't care about the heat. She didn't care about the cotton she was cleaning. All she wanted was for her father and her uncles and cousins to climb into their bateaus and go find Paul.

The back door banged open, and Papa came in carrying an armload of firewood. "Will supper be ready soon?"

Maman nodded. "I put the fish in just after you began chopping wood. It won't be long." As she spoke she went to the hearth and used a pot rag to lift the heavy lid. She poked at the gumbo with her wooden spoon, then touched it to her lips.

Maman smiled up at Papa. "Very soon. Just time enough to wash up."

He nodded at her and headed for the pitcher and basin that stood on a low cypress table against the back wall. Lily plucked at the cottonseed, her movements jerky with anger. They were just going to pretend nothing was wrong. And they expected her to do the same.

"Help me, Lily," Rose Eva called in her soft voice.

"Help you what?" Lily snapped, feeling raw and upset.

"Help me sew." Rose Eva stuck out her lower lip. Her cheeks were flushed with the heat. She looked like one of the angels in 'Nonc Jean's Bible.

Lily tried to smile. "All right." She stood up and dusted the cotton lint from her hands and skirt. Her first step was awkward, her weak ankle cramped from sitting cross-legged. She bumped into her father, and he caught her by the shoulders, holding her tightly until she had her balance again.

Without a word, he kissed the top of her head, then went past her. She limped to Rose Eva and sank to the floor beside her. Rose Eva made her pouting face again and handed Lily a hopeless tangle of thread and puckered cloth.

Marie looked aside, her mouth twitching, and Lily knew she was trying not to laugh. Rose Eva knew it too, and she got to her feet and stomped to the back door, reaching up to pull the leather handle as she let herself out.

"She's terrible at sewing," Marie said, then giggled.

"She's only three," Lily heard herself say in a cold, angry voice.

"What is the matter with you?" Maman said, still stirring the gumbo.

Lily got up, her ankle still aching. "Nothing," she said, then went out the front door to stand alone on the gallerie, biting her lip. After a few minutes, she turned to go back in, then stopped herself. Papa and Maman would never understand. But Paul was her friend, and she was going to figure out a way to help him.

Walking toward the bayou, Lily glanced toward the lowering sun. There were five families within a mile, and she was related to them all. She thought frantically, trying to figure out who would take her word that Paul Courville was worthy of help.

The sun settled onto the horizon. Its slanting light was shattered by the locust trees Papa had planted years before. Staring into the sunset, Lily admitted to herself that no one she knew would be any more willing than her own father to help a plantation family. There were just too many hard feelings against the wealthy planters. If she wanted to help Paul, it was up to her to do it alone.

Chapter Eight

Paul sat against the tree. His skin was still on fire, stinging and itching from the mosquito bites. He was terrified. The sun was lowering in the west, and he had shouted for help until his voice failed. He did not want to spend another night cramped and aching in the tree. He had no idea what could have happened to his brothers, but he knew something was terribly wrong.

Paul licked his lips and toed at the branch he had broken from the tree. He was sick with thirst and hunger. After the alligator had disappeared, carrying the duck away, Paul had climbed down out of the tree, his legs cramped and shaking. He had tried all day to kill one of the ducks, but every time he had gotten close enough to swing the branch, they had flown. He was clumsy with fatigue, and he was beginning to think he might not live through this.

A big snake slid out of the grass, and Paul blinked, jolted from his despairing thoughts. He froze, pressing his back hard against the tree, swallowing painfully. The snake stopped, lifting its coppery-brown head, its tongue flicking in and out.

It was light brown and patterned like dappled sunlight. Paul was afraid to breathe. This was a copperhead, one of the most poisonous snakes in the swamp. He watched, his eyes stinging as sweat ran from his forehead. The snake stretched out, sunning itself. Paul held himself still, his heart thundering inside his chest, his breath uneven and shallow. The snake rested its wide head on the ground, moving only when a sudden breeze bent the grass. Then it lowered its head again.

Suddenly unable to control his fear, Paul sprang to his feet. Clawing at the bark, he managed to clamber upward, reclaiming his night's perch. He balanced on the branch, trying to accept that he had made it, that the snake had not attacked him. He was incredibly lucky. Instead of striking, the snake had moved back a little, coiling at the edge of the thick grass.

Paul stayed as still as he could, helplessly staring at the snake. As afraid as he was, every moment that passed brought back the weight of his fatigue and hunger. He found himself yawning, leaning forward on the branch. The snake did not move. Its slick scales glittered in the late sunlight.

A copperhead bite would kill him, Paul knew. He had heard stories about cottonmouths and copperheads all his life and once or twice he had seen ones the slaves had killed in the cane. But those lifeless, slack-skinned carcasses were nothing like the muscular, menacing shape below him.

Suddenly the snake seemed to sense Paul's presence. It raised its head and arched its body into a tight curve, whipping around so it faced the tree. Paul held his breath. He had no idea if the snake could see him or not, but it seemed to be looking straight at him.

Its sinewy body coiled and tense, the snake flicked its tongue in and out of its mouth. Paul let his breath out soundlessly and pulled in another. Sweat trickled down his temples, and his hands were slimy with it.

Paul lifted his right hand from the tree branch, intending to wipe it on his trouser leg. The snake reacted instantly to his movement. It slithered in a straight line, coming directly toward the tree trunk, its head raised.

Paul clambered to his feet, grasping at a narrow branch overhead to keep his balance. The copperhead twisted, opening its mouth and hissing. Paul flinched backward involuntarily, and his right foot slid off the limb. His sweaty hands slipped on the tree bark, sending a jolt through his whole body. Unable to keep his balance, his heart slamming against his ribs, he pitched sideways. His right leg hooked over the branch, and he swung, dangling upside down.

Reaching up to grab at the limb, Paul was dizzied by the blur of grass and dark water below him. Clutching the rough bark, he craned his neck to look down. The snake was directly below him now, its body arched into a hostile question mark.

Paul hauled himself upward as well as he could, clinging to the underside of the branch. He could not stop looking at the snake, could not stop the trembling in his arms and legs. If he fell, the snake would strike.

Forcing himself to concentrate, knowing his life depended on it, Paul pulled in a deep breath, then hitched his weight to one side, clamping his knees against the limb. He took in a few breaths, then did it again. Inch by inch, acutely aware of the copperhead coiled a dozen feet below, Paul managed to pull himself around to the top of the branch.

Collapsing in relief, he lay still for a long time, wrapped around the limb. Trembling, he kept his eyes closed. He had never in his life come that close to dying, and it had left him feeling hollow.

After a long moment, Paul was finally able to open his eyes and focus on the ground. He blinked back tears of disbelief. The snake was gone. Pushing himself upright, he sat, straddling the limb. He saw a movement from the corner of his eye and turned to see the last handspan of the snake's body disappear beneath the dark water of the swamp.

Shaking from head to foot as the sun sat on the horizon, Paul tried to think clearly. The night before he had been miserable. It was impossible to rest in the tree, much less sleep.

"I should have struck out for home," he said aloud. "I should have started off first thing this morning and just kept going."

The sound of his own voice was strange and

unsettling in his ears. Somewhere in the distance there was a long, screeching call he didn't recognize. He knew he was only a couple of hours away from his parents' polished wood floor and spotless white mosquito netting. He was so close to his own bed, with its smooth, clean linens.

He was sure there was a rescue party looking for him. He had heard stories all his life about how easily people got lost in the bayou country, but he had never had any idea until now how true it was.

Paul crouched on the limb as the sun sank. He would strike out tomorrow. "In which direction?" he asked himself, speaking aloud again.

"Help me!" Paul yelled without meaning to. He stood up, bracing one leg against the trunk to steady himself. "Someone help me!"

His throat was raw from shouting, but he could not seem to keep himself from doing it. As long as the sound of his own voice was echoing around him, it held back the fear. Breathing as hard as if he had been running, Paul finally forced himself to stop. It was useless now. No one would be looking for him at night.

Paul slumped against the tree trunk, embracing it.

The sun was going down, haloed in red light through the cypress trees. Paul's heart sank with it. He ground his teeth together, holding back another cry for help.

Lily could not sleep. She lay still with her eyes closed, but her thoughts were churning. Papa and Maman had not said another word about the Courville brothers. Papa had done all he would when he had offered Mr. Thomas his help.

"And what do I expect him to do?" Lily whispered to herself in the dark. "Order a plantation boss to let him help search?"

Lily heard Marie shift on her cot, making the dreamy little sleep-sound Lily was so familiar with, but she did not awaken. Rose Eva did not stir either. Once she had begun sleeping through the night as a baby, she had become the deepest dreamer in the family. Nothing woke her, not even thunder.

Lily sighed and sat up on her cot and held very still, listening to her sisters' soft breathing. Paul's mother would be frantic. Lily tried to imagine how Maman would feel if Augustin and Pierre were lost. She tried to imagine how *she* would feel.

Without really meaning to, Lily swung her feet to

the cool plank floor. She stood up slowly, afraid to admit to herself what she was doing. Even when she pulled her chemise and dress from the hooks beside the door, she was telling herself that she only meant to go outside for a while, to walk the gallerie until she was tired enough to sleep.

Lily eased open her bedroom door. The leather hinges made no sound at all. Her bare feet were equally silent on the planked floor. There was a little glow still in the hearth to light her way, and her parents' door was closed tightly. She tiptoed past it.

Lily spooned pieces of fish from the gumbo into a clean cloth. Then she wrapped what remained of the evening's corn bread. She took a piece of salt pork and some rice, too, and she placed everything in her mother's oldest flour sack.

She took down a shawl from the clothes hooks by the hearth, and thought about taking her shoes. But it was not likely she would end up inside the Courvilles' house, and in the swamp, shoes were only in the way.

Lily got one of her father's waterskins and filled it from the kitchen bucket. Then she quietly opened the cypress box that held the knives. Picking out her skinning blade, she dropped it into the sack too.

Bracing her shoulders, Lily went out the front door. There was no way to rebar it, and she hesitated on the gallerie. Then she said a prayer for her family's safety and turned resolutely toward the landing. There was a big moon rising, and she was grateful. A dark night would have been much worse.

Lily's pirogue seemed to be waiting patiently for her. She climbed into it, thinking about her grandfather. She often imagined he was still alive, paddling in the bow, insisting she learn to steer from the stern.

Shivering a little, Lily lowered her sack into the pirogue. Then she untied the mooring rope and climbed in. She picked up her paddle and settled herself on the bench. Then she wrapped her shawl around her neck and head, using the ends to tie it.

Straightening her back and holding the paddle tightly, Lily lowered it into the water. Using quick back strokes, tilting the paddle so it didn't splash, she moved her pirogue away from the landing. Then she turned it and started off into the night.

Chapter Nine

Paul was crouched on the branch, trembling with cold. The mosquitoes had gotten worse as the night went on. Now, close to dawn, he had given up trying to swat them away. Their whining buzz rang in his ears, and their needlelike stings tortured him.

The horizon was getting lighter. Paul kept staring at it, trying to fix the direction in his mind. He knew that within a few hours, the sun would be an elusive glare, sifted through the canopy of the trees and moss. A soft splash in the water riveted his attention. The dawn-dusk was still so thick, he couldn't make out anything, not even a shape. But the sound had been close. He strained to hear.

For a long time there was only silence and the distant sound of birdcalls. Paul's legs ached from being cramped. His arms were sore from holding on, and the palms of his hands hurt from scraping against the bark of the tree. As he had so many times during the night, Paul fought his fears to a standstill.

"The minute it is light enough, I will start out."

Paul was startled by his own rough whisper. His throat was painfully dry, and he was so thirsty that the thought of clear water was overwhelming. He had drunk a little of the fetid bayou water the day before. It had made his stomach churn and ache, but he would have to drink more of it soon, he was sure.

"And I have to eat soon."

Saying this aloud made Paul laugh bitterly. Was there any reason to assume his duck-hunting skills would have improved overnight? He dragged his tongue across his teeth, trying to work up some saliva. He couldn't. His tongue was so dry, it stuck to the roof of his mouth.

The irony of being so thirsty in the center of flooded land hit Paul hard, and he began to laugh again. Then, he shook his head and tried to change his grip on the slender branch above his head. Abruptly, his laughter died in his throat. His cramped hand would not open.

◊ ◊ ◊

Lily came into Bayou Teche just as the sun broke free of the eastern horizon. She had been paddling hard, shooting the pirogue through the tight passages of Bayou LeGrand. She knew it so well that with only a little moonlight, she had felt safe in hurrying. The mosquitoes were bad, as always, but she had wrapped the long, fringed shawl about her neck and face. The insects had raised welts on her forearms and ankles, but she was used to that.

She had come upon only one *cocodrie*. It had been a small one that slithered out of the water as she had paddled past. She had veered to the far side of the bayou, then angled back to the center again.

Alligators were all through the swamp, especially in the deeper channels and pools. But on Bayou LeGrand, her uncles and cousins had been hunting them for fifty years, so there were fewer here than in other places. No one wanted alligators living too close to their farms; they sometimes ate pigs and dogs.

Bayou Teche seemed as wide as an ocean after the narrow confines of Bayou LeGrand. The towering cypresses that lined the banks were like ghosts in the moonlight, robed in Spanish moss. The levees were well kept and high, and she could not see the mansions she knew were there, or the endless fields of last fall's sugarcane, standing thick and high and ready for harvest.

Lily paddled at a measured pace as the sun rose in the east. She still had quite a ways to go to get to Fair Oaks. She kept glancing behind herself. When Papa saw she was gone, he would come after her. He would be furious at her disobedience. So would Maman. It would be a long time before they allowed her to use her pirogue again. Papa might even take it away from her and give it to the boys.

Lily stroked the smooth hull, thinking about her grandfather. He had loved his children and grand-children. He had been an honest man and had been good to his friends. He would understand her need to try to help Paul, she was sure.

"And I wish you were alive, *Grand-père*," she whispered. He could have helped her make Papa understand.

The first rays of sunlight flashed through the trees, low and slanting. Lily leaned into her paddle, pulling hard.

"Hey, you! Girl!"

Lily turned to see a man standing on the levee, waving his arms in a wide arc above his head. She back-paddled and turned the pirogue to face him. "Me?"

The man nodded, an exaggerated gesture. "You! Have you seen three boys out in the swamps somewhere?"

Lily shook her head, unwilling to explain to this stranger that one of the missing boys was her friend.

"You're a Cajun, ain't you?" the man shouted. He said the last word in an odd, cramped way that told her he did not like her people. She inclined her head. Not exactly a nod, but almost.

"Thought so," the man shouted across the still, dark water at her. "Well, have you seen them or not?"

Lily shook her head again, then glanced behind her, even though she knew Papa would just now be rising and it would be an hour or two more before he could get to where she was now.

"Hey, girl! I asked you a question."

"No, sir," Lily shouted back, "I have not seen them. Do you know how long they have been missing?"

The man shook his head violently, another overblown gesture for her benefit. "I only heard about it this morning. You keep an eye out, you hear me? And if you find them up this way, you can bring them here if any of them are in a bad way."

"Thank you, sir," Lily shouted as she dug her paddle deeply into the water, turning her pirogue downstream. As she went on, she forced herself to stop glancing behind her every few seconds. It would only slow her down. Everything depended on not letting Papa catch up with her.

As the sun slowly rose higher in the sky, Lily kept up her pace. The plantations slid past on either side, and she could hear the palmettos rattling as a breeze kicked up. She was grateful. It would blow some of the flies and mosquitoes away. The day would soon be very warm, and she would be glad to untie the shawl around her neck.

Lily kept her paddle strokes long and even, constantly seeking out the places where the slow current was strongest and would help push her pirogue along. As she drew close to the Courville plantation, she slowed a little and kept to the opposite bank. She longed to ask someone if the boys had been found, but she hated to reveal herself too. Papa would ask after her here, she was sure.

"And how big a fool will you be if you go searching and they are all safe at home?" Lily asked herself.

Still, when she saw Mr. Thomas shouting instructions to levee workers, she paddled into the deepest shadows she could find and glided by silently.

At the far edge of Fair Oaks, Lily saw spires of sooty black smoke rising into the sky. Slaves were burning off the cane fields. She hesitated, lifting her paddle from the sluggish water. Her pirogue slowed instantly.

Listening, Lily heard singing. Paul had told her once that the slaves rarely sang when Mr. Thomas was nearby. If they knew he was preoccupied on the levee, Lily thought, maybe one of them could tell her what had happened.

Staying in the dense shade, paddling closely around the stands of cypress and the tall tupelo gums that grew on a wide sandbar, Lily crossed the river. She ran her pirogue aground in a clump of willows at the toe of the levee.

Then, doubling over to make herself harder to see, she struggled up the slope, hesitating long enough at the top to look around for Mr. Thomas. When she didn't see him, she dropped low again and crept closer, her limp exaggerated by her awkward position.

She spotted Jedediah standing at the edge of the field, and she hesitated. Even though he and Papa were friendly, Jedediah was a slave, and she wasn't sure he would risk punishment by talking to her about the Courvilles. Lily watched him for a moment as he walked out of the field toward the water bucket that stood in the center of the road. When he raised the drinking gourd to his lips, Lily whispered his name.

Jedediah turned, scanning the brush. She lifted her head, just high enough so that he could see her. Watching his reaction carefully, she was poised to run back to her pirogue. She did not want to be found out, or mean to cause any trouble for him.

Jedediah sidled toward her, glancing around. "What is it, missy?"

"Have they found Paul?"

Jedediah shook his head. "Nor the other two."

Lily felt her stomach tighten and she realized how much she had been hoping that Paul was already safe. Now she had no choice, no matter how much trouble it caused.

"You going to look for him?"

Lily nodded. "Paul's not like his brothers."

"Out of that batch, he's surely the best one," Jedediah agreed. "I saw them as far as the island above LaSalle's landing."

"Thank you, Jedediah," she said.

He didn't answer.

"Please don't tell anyone I was here," she begged him.

He turned just enough to meet her eyes. She saw him nod, a barely perceptible motion that no one else could possibly notice. Then he turned and walked toward the burning cane.

Lily drew back into the bushes and turned, her uneven stride carrying her down the slope to her pirogue. She pushed it into the water and waded out knee-deep, climbing awkwardly over the side. She reached for her paddle before she was seated on the bench. Then, paddling hard, she kept to the shadows as much as she could as she started down the bayou toward LaSalle's landing.

Paul stood beside his tree, swaying and dizzy, scanning the grass. His eyes were nearly swollen shut. The sunrise looked to him like a teary haze of red and gold. He was dizzy with hunger. His hands were numb from gripping the limb, and he could not straighten his cramped legs.

The grass was still—no snakes. Paul wiped at his eyes with his sleeve, and the mosquito bites flared into a stinging itch he could barely stand. Walking crookedly, crashing to his knees at the edge of the narrow channel, Paul leaned forward and managed to splash a little of the brown water onto his face.

It trickled across his lips, and before he could stop himself, he was bent over, drinking like a cow at a trough, swallowing as fast as he could. For a moment, Paul could only feel the soothing passage of the water down his throat, but then he brought himself back to reason and raised his head. The water had made him queasy the day before. He knew it was foolish to drink much of it.

Staggering back to his feet, Paul fought for his balance. His head ached, and he resisted the urge to wipe at his eyes again. He squeezed them shut, then opened them, and the world looked a little clearer.

Paul was so hungry that his stomach was clenched tight. He heard a soft splashing and saw ducks swimming not far away. He longed for a gun, then laughed aloud. He was too shaky to shoot straight.

His laughter startled the ducks into flight, and he watched them go, sadness in his heart.

"I was going to set off for home this morning," Paul reminded himself, hauling in a deep breath. He took a single step forward, then another. He walked unsteadily to the edge of the channel, then stood there, peering into the dark brown water. He inched forward, meaning to go slowly, but the bank was too steep. He slipped in the mud and skidded downward, unable to stop himself. His scalp prickled as the water closed over him and he felt the soft-mud bottom of the channel beneath his feet.

Paul half swam, half stood, managing to get his head above the surface. He dragged in a breath the instant he could, his heart racing. He hated the brown water. He hated that he wouldn't be able to see an alligator or a snake.

Paul tried to wade out, his jacket and vest weighing him down. Suddenly, he felt something slide along his neck and he whirled in the water, striking out and shouting. His numbed fingers closed on something, and he floundered in the water, trying to let go of it, to fling it away from himself. A sharp pain in his cheek brought him back to reality. He stopped shouting and lowered his hands, standing still in the dark water.

Paul groaned aloud. There was no snake. He was holding a stick and had jabbed himself in the face with the end of it. Shaking, his heart still pounding inside his chest, he managed to swim awkwardly back to the bank.

Laboriously, his breathing coming hard, Paul climbed out of the water, stumbled, and fell to his knees in the mud. Finally, he dragged himself upright and stood in the early sun, his face bleeding. He touched the cut. It wasn't deep, but it hurt, and Paul shook his head, imagining what he must have looked like, fighting the stick-snake to the death. He wondered if he would ever be able to tell anyone about it. Even if he made it out of the swamp alive, he couldn't think of a single person he would be able to trust not to laugh at him.

Maybe Lily, he thought after a moment. She had been laughed at her whole life because of her crippled foot. She would understand. Paul sank down beside his tree, promising himself he would rise soon and wade the channel again. If he stayed where he was, he was going to die of hunger.

Chapter Ten

As Lily started around a long curve in the waterway, the sound of a steamboat whistle made her look up. The wide, flat-bottomed boat was churning its way straight toward her. She could see people standing on the decks. There were dark-suited men, and two or three women with plumed hats.

Lily looked upriver, gauging the speed of the steamer. A little ways ahead, where it would pass her, the channel got so narrow, there would be barely enough room for the paddle wheeler to pass through. That meant the people on deck would be looking straight down into her pirogue.

There was no doubt in Lily's mind they would all notice the odd sight of a girl by herself on the bayou. And some of them would talk about it to their neighbors. Lily knew her chances of getting away with all this were very slim, but the fewer people who saw her, the better.

Lily put her paddle back into the water. Dragging hard with each stroke, she veered toward the opposite shore. Just ahead, there was a low-lying island with cattails thick around it like ruffles on the hem of a skirt. It jutted out far enough that steamboats had to make their way around it, sticking to the deeper channel.

Intent on staying hidden, and out of the way of the wake of the steam-driven paddle wheels, Lily maneuvered into water so shallow, her pirogue ground its bottom on sand and came to a clumsy stop.

Leaning forward, lying low in the bottom of her boat, Lily waited for the steamboat to go past. Then she sat up and tried stabbing her paddle into the mud and shoving backward. It didn't work.

Lily was afraid to get out of her pirogue, but she knew she had no choice. It was tilted dangerously to one side, and she knew there was no hope of pushing it back into water deep enough to paddle again.

Hitching up her skirts, Lily eased her weight onto her strong right foot, sinking almost up to her knee in the mud. She felt something wriggle beneath her foot and shifted her weight quickly, hoping she hadn't hurt the frog. She was afraid, but she resolved not to let herself think about what could happen to her if she became mired in the mud. She would not allow it to happen, she promised herself. She knew what to do.

Swinging her left leg over the side of her pirogue, she leaned forward, shoving at the boat as she took her weight out of it. The pirogue slid back into water just deep enough to float it.

Lily could feel the mud molding itself to her legs as she sank deeper. Still holding on to the prow of the boat, she hitched her skirt higher and fell forward. By letting her hands and knees share her weight, she managed to free herself from the pull of the soft mud, crawling across it, shoving the pirogue inch by inch, farther into deep water.

Her dress filthy, she waded in up to her thighs, then heaved herself over the side of her little boat and lay still for a moment, listening to the sound of her heart. People died by making such foolish mistakes. She sat up and scooped water into her hands to rinse her face. Then, her mouth set in a grim line, she started forward again, this time watching carefully ahead and guiding her pirogue more slowly through the water.

Because she was so intent on watching the depth, it took a moment for Lily to pick out the little patch of unnatural white from the tangle of dead leaves that floated on the still water. When she did, she paddled carefully toward it and leaned out to lift it with the tip of her oar.

Spreading the handkerchief across her knee, she saw a familiar monogram. Her heart beating faster, she scanned the cattails in the shallow water. There. The tall, green stalks had been bent. It was a fairly wide swath. She had not asked whether the boys had been in a pirogue or a flat-bottomed bateau—now she knew.

Excited to have found a sign so quickly, Lily angled her pirogue. Now it would be up to her to notice more signs in the swamp, and most of them would be far less apparent. She took a deep breath and began to paddle again.

Paul opened his eyes. His clothes were damp and muddy. He had no idea what had happened. He had no memory of deciding to nap or rest. His thoughts seemed to circle slowly. He rubbed at his face and was startled by the painful itch of the mosquito bites.

He sat up, blinking, scanning the ground near the tree. He looked into every sunlit clump of grass, every tangle of creeper vines. He held as still as death, barely breathing.

Only once Paul was sure there were no snakes close by did he struggle to his feet. He glanced up, seeing a glint of white-gold sunlight overhead. A few hours had gone past, of that much he was sure—maybe more. The sun was near its zenith now. Even though he could not see it through the thick canopy, it was obvious the shattered rays were coming from nearly straight overhead.

Paul could remember lying down, but that was all. For a long moment, he stared at the dark bayou water and felt his belly cramp as he recalled lying down to drink. Looking at the muddy, stagnant water, he shuddered. He didn't want to drink any more of it and he didn't want to wade into it again. In a flash, he remembered sliding down the muddy bank and the terror of the stick that had bumped his hand. He lowered his head.

He stood for a long time, then lifted his eyes and took a deep breath. He was weak with hunger and he knew it was only going to get worse. He forced himself to take a step toward the water. His knees felt like wooden blocks, and his feet ached. Every step hurt. When he came to the edge of the water, he stopped.

He squeezed his swollen eyes shut and opened them again. Then, careful not to slip this time, he waded cautiously into the water. It got deeper as he went. He shivered as it inched up his body until he was chest deep in the channel. Swallowing hard, praying there were no snakes beneath the dark surface, he kept going, his eyes fixed on a trio of gum trees.

Expecting to feel the sharp stab of poisonous fangs any second, Paul made himself keep wading. Slowly, the water became more shallow, and he rejoiced as it inched back down to his waist, then his thighs, then his boot tops.

Blinking back tears of relief, he waded out, sucking in the warm, damp air with a reverence he had never felt in church. He was weak and hungry, and he was still afraid, but he would no longer let his fear paralyze him. He had to find the way home.

A sudden rush of wings overhead made Paul whirl around, looking upward. Egrets swooped over him, then angled low over the water, their snow-white tails floating out behind them. He had always thought they were beautiful. He had always loved seeing them when they landed in the flooded rice fields at home. Now, all he could think about was finding a way to knock one out of the sky so he could pluck it and eat it raw.

Wildly, Paul turned, searching the ground around him for sticks or rocks. A second wave of egrets passed overhead, and he clenched his fists, frantic to find something he could throw. Two snow-white stragglers passed above him as his right hand closed around a thick chunk of rotten wood.

Reaching back and flinging the wood as hard as he could, Paul cried out. He shouted again as the wood fell pitifully short and splashed back into the swamp. He cursed, kicking at a clump of grass, then lurching to one side when he lost his balance. He had to eat soon. No matter what it took, he had to find a way to eat. His mouth flooded with saliva at the thought of food, but his mind forced him back to reality.

"And how would you clean it?" he asked himself as

he sat down heavily to pull off his boots and empty out the water inside. "With what? Your fingernails?"

Paul shivered, even though it was a hot day. He stared out at the jumbled tangle of trees and vines. The gum trees were wrapped in creepers as big around as his arm. As he stared, he saw a flash of green against the bark and realized it was a snake, threading its way upward through the vines.

The air, filled with the smell of rotting leaves and the heavy scent of fetid water, suddenly seemed too thick to breathe. "William!" Paul shouted, his throat sore and dry. "Mark!" His cries faded into nothing. Wherever his brothers were, Paul knew they could not hear him.

Paul made himself start walking. He had no idea which way to go, and he knew, deep in his heart, that he had no real chance of getting out of the swamp alive. But he refused to lie down again. If he was going to die, he would die walking.

Chapter Eleven

Paul walked woodenly through the eerie gloom of the swamp. Twice he scared up snakes that slithered away from him. Both times, his heart thudded, slowing only once he had walked on.

He waded the channels he came to, then walked on dry ground as far as he could, trying to keep to a westerly course. It was hard. The sunshine seemed to come from every direction, and from nowhere at all. He stumbled along, refusing to stop even though his thoughts were reeling.

The Cajuns had stories, he knew. They believed there were strange haunts and grotesque creatures that lived in places like this. His parents didn't give credence to the stories, but they had their own. His mother had told him once about a man named Coco who headed a family of criminals and half-wild children somewhere north on the Teche. He was a dangerous man who was said to kill even harmless intruders.

An abrupt splash in the water off to his right jerked Paul around, and he stared into the shadows. A fan of ripples guided his eye, and he was startled into stillness. There, swimming toward him, was an alligator. It swam low in the water, only its leathery snout and head rising above the surface.

Paul stood rooted for a few seconds more, then he backed up, step by shaking step. The alligator kept coming.

"Run!"

The voice seemed to come from some other world, and Paul at first did not understand it was directed at him.

"Paul! Run!"

He turned and stumbled forward, almost falling, then managed to stagger upright.

"This way!"

He veered toward the sound of the voice and saw Lily. She was standing on solid ground, but just beyond her, he saw her pirogue. He glanced behind himself.

"It's not chasing you," Lily called. "Don't be afraid."

Slowing down, stumbling and heavy-footed, Paul kept walking, his eyes fixed on Lily's face. He couldn't believe she was here. Paul let Lily grasp his arm, helping him into the pirogue. "Move back," she said. "Balance our weight."

Paul managed to do as she said. A second later, he felt the pirogue move backward. Maneuvering it deftly, Lily glanced back.

"Where are your brothers?"

The question startled Paul, and he opened his mouth, then closed it again, uncertain what to say. "So they didn't make it home," he answered finally.

"I talked to Jedediah this morning," Lily said, turning to glance at him again without breaking the rhythm of her paddling. "He said you were all still lost."

"He would know if they'd been found," Paul told her, his spirits sinking.

"What were you doing out here?" Lily asked.

Paul could not find an answer he was willing to give. "Thank you," he said, ignoring her question. He pulled in a breath. Those two words could not begin to carry the gratitude he felt. "My father will be grateful too," he began.

"Mine won't," Lily interrupted. "He'll be furious."

Paul sat up straighter, trying to make his thoughts march in a row. Of course. Why would her father want him saved? And why was she here alone? The two questions seemed to answer each other, and he stared at the back of Lily's head.

She had an old shawl tied around her waist, and her glossy dark hair curled down her back. She wasn't wearing the bonnet he sometimes saw her in. "Your father doesn't know you're here, does he?" Paul asked.

Lily shook her head without answering.

"You saved my life," Paul said. He didn't know what else to say.

"There's water," she said, pointing.

The simple, beautiful sound of the word "water" lifted Paul's spirits.

"And there's food in the bag behind you."

Paul followed her gesture and found himself shaking. "Thank you," he rasped. "I am so hungry . . . " He trailed off, unable to finish the sentence.

She turned around. "When did you eat last?"

"I don't know," he told her. "Right before they brought me out here. But that was—"

"What do you mean 'they brought' you? Who? Mark and William?" Lily was staring at him, and he wanted to respond, but all he could think about was the caved-in hollow in his belly. He reached for the sack and unwrapped the soggy corn bread. He stuffed it into his mouth and nearly choked getting it down.

"Here."

Paul looked up to see Lily looking at him. She had laid the paddle down and was holding the waterskin. She undid the thong and pinched the opening closed, holding it out to him. He took it, his hands shaking. Lily steadied the waterskin as he tipped it up.

The cool feel of clean water in his mouth was incredible. He gulped it down, stopping only when Lily gently tugged the skin away. As she replaced the leather tie, he crammed more of the corn bread into his mouth. When he looked up, she was smiling at him.

"You are going to live."

He managed a nod. "I didn't think so an hour ago, but I do now."

Lily's smile widened into a grin. "Your mother and father will be so glad to see you." She reached for her paddle.

"Wait," Paul said.

She hesitated, an odd look on her face. "For what?"

"William and Mark must be out here somewhere." He said it slowly, watching her expression.

She frowned. "Your father will find them. Maybe he already has."

Paul was unable to think of anything to say, but he knew he had to convince her. "But we can't leave without looking for them."

Lily lifted her chin high. "I owed you. Not them." She picked up her paddle again, then lowered it into the water and took the first stroke. As the pirogue moved beneath them, Paul leaned forward to stop her. "Please, Lily. They didn't bring food or water." He could see her struggling with her feelings.

"Your brothers," she said in a low voice, "are both bullies and they've never been anything but cruel to me."

Paul nodded. "It's true, but I—" He paused. Some of the hollow dizziness had passed. He felt a little stronger now. The cramped aching in his belly was letting up. He reached for the waterskin and took another drink. "They are my brothers," he said. "I can't just leave them here."

Lily shifted around to sit facing him. "Tell me how you got here."

He shook his head, afraid if he told her the truth, she would insist on leaving.

"Tell me."

Paul's stomach tightened as he explained. He could see she was close to tears.

"I have always hated your brothers."

"I know," Paul said, looking aside. He couldn't defend William and Mark. But he couldn't leave them, either.

"They would leave me."

Startled by the intensity of Lily's voice, Paul looked up and met her eyes. "No they wouldn't. They never meant for anyone to get hurt. It was just one of their tricks."

Lily stared into his eyes for a long time before she spoke again. "I have to be home by nightfall."

"Thank you, Lily," Paul said gravely, relieved she had given in.

Lily wasn't entirely sure why she had agreed to stay, but she knew she didn't want to stay a second longer than she had to. "Which way did they go when they left you?"

She watched Paul turn one way, then the other, looking out over the swamp. He finally shook his head. "Lily, I don't know. I'm not even sure which way I walked today."

Lily sighed, wishing he could at least help her pick a direction to start in.

"William!" Paul bellowed suddenly, startling her. He cupped his hands around his mouth. "Mark!"

The vast silence of the swamp absorbed his cries, and the only answer was the rush of wings overhead. A flock of birds had been alarmed into flight.

Lily looked at Paul, pitying him. His poor face was so swollen, and she could tell he was exhausted and weak. His voice sounded raw and hoarse. Still, she could see he was taking in another big breath and sitting up straighter. He cupped his hands around his mouth and faced the opposite direction.

"William! Mark!"

Lily was frantic to begin searching. Paul didn't understand the risk she was taking, and she didn't know how to explain it to him. Her father could find them, at any moment, and if he did, he would be angry that she was alone with Paul again. When he told her uncles and aunts how improper her behavior had been, her whole family would think less of her. And it wasn't just any boy: Paul was a planter's son!

It would be no better if search parties from Fair Oaks came upon them. The Courvilles might assume she had had something to do with the twins disappearing. Everyone knew how they taunted her, how much Cajuns hated the planter families who had bought up their *petit habitants*, forcing them to move.

"William! Maaaark!"

Lily thought she heard a faint cry.

"Did you hear that?" Paul asked.

Lily nodded. "I think so. It might have been a bird."

Paul stood up in the pirogue. It tipped to one side.

"Sit down!" Lily warned him.

He glanced at her, nodding, setting his feet wider apart. Then he lifted his head and shouted again.

This time, as the sound of his voice faded, there was a chattering of birdsong from overhead. Paul grimaced angrily and clenched his fists. As soon as the birds quieted down, he shouted once more.

Lily listened intently. There it was again. It was faint, and she knew it could be a bird. But the timing of the answer made her think it wasn't.

"Did you hear it?" Paul asked.

Lily nodded. "Yes. But it could have been—"

"A bird," Paul finished for her. "But it wasn't. It's them."

He shouted once more, and Lily heard the answer more clearly this time. She picked up her paddle and began to row.

Chapter Twelve

Paul yelled his brothers' names again.

"Sit down," Lily ordered over her shoulder.

Paul sank awkwardly onto the narrow plank bench, the pirogue swaying beneath his feet as his weight shifted. "Sorry." He said it softly, then fell silent, listening intently. The cry had been so faint that even the muted sound of water swirling against Lily's paddle made it hard to hear. "Over there," he said when it came again.

Lily nodded but didn't speak.

Silent seconds ticked by as the pirogue glided over the dark water. Lily maneuvered the boat gracefully—and faster than he could believe. She seemed to know where the water would be deep enough, even where grass grew just inches away.

Paul framed his mouth with his hands and shouted again. But this time, he couldn't hear an answer. "Did you hear them?" he asked Lily.

She shook her head without turning.

Paul closed his eyes, straining to catch even the faintest response. When it didn't come, he shouted once more. "William! Mark!"

This time, Lily stopped paddling, lifting her oar out of the water. Paul tried to still even his breathing as he listened. There was no answer. Paul's heart was thudding, and he half stood without thinking, tilting the pirogue.

"Stay down!" Lily whispered harshly.

He mumbled an apology, feeling foolish. His head had cleared a little, but the fatigue in his body still seemed to slow his thinking.

"There?" Lily asked, pointing to their right.

Paul lifted his head. "I didn't hear anything that time."

Lily spoke without turning. "Try again."

Paul shouted, straining his lungs. He tried to make his voice penetrate the heavy air of the swamp, but it seemed to him that his cry dissolved under the weight of the humid air even faster. Still, a few seconds after silence had settled around them, a tiny cry came from somewhere off to their right.

"I thought so," Lily said as she began to paddle.

Paul sat still, amazed at how Lily threaded a route from one narrow channel to another. They rounded stands of live oak, draped with curtains of silvery Spanish moss. She guided the little boat between ancient cypresses with root knees taller than a grown man.

"Call your brothers," Lily said after a few minutes.

Paul yelled as loud as he could. This time the answer came quicker, and it was a little louder. Lily started forward again.

The maze of the swamp made Paul uneasy: He hated not having any idea which direction he had come from, or where they should be headed. He tried to guess Lily's path as they went, the dark water sliding beneath the pirogue. But he could not. Every twenty or thirty feet, Lily had to work the pirogue through a tangle of vines, turning, then turning again to find water deep enough to keep going. Yet, somehow, she seemed not to lose her way.

"Shout," Lily said. Then she pointed. "That way."

Paul faced the direction she indicated and called

out his brothers' names as loudly as he could.

This time, the answer was much louder, and it was no longer a cry. It had become human speech: "Over here!"

"William?" Paul blurted. Then he raised his voice back to a shout and called his brothers' names once more.

"I think I see them," Lily said. She held out the paddle, using it to point a way through the green labyrinth of trees and vines. Then she moved the pirogue forward.

Paul squinted, rubbing his swollen eyes. He couldn't pick out anything from the mosaic of blinding sun and shadowy darkness at first. Then, as Lily paddled them along, he heard his brothers shouting. He leaned out to see around Lily, and there they were in the distance, two stick figures waving frantically.

Lily shook her head. "They were headed *south*? For New Orleans?"

Paul found himself smiling in spite of the pain it caused in his swollen face. "My father will thank you for this," he told Lily. "Maybe there will even be a reward."

Lily turned far enough to flash him a dirty look. "I did not do this in hope of being paid."

"I didn't mean to insult you," Paul said quickly. "I just thought—"

"Mon Dieu!"

The tone of astonishment in her voice hushed him instantly. He leaned aside again, peering around her as she speeded her paddling. What he saw frightened him. His brothers were not standing on solid land as he had thought. They were clinging to the tangled vines that encased two tall trees. William was ten or twelve feet above the ground. Mark was just above him. Below them was the biggest alligator Paul had ever seen. It was looking up at them, its jaws wide enough to show its teeth.

"Mon Dieu." This time Lily said it very softly, and her voice was almost drowned out in the bellowing call of the enraged animal. As the alligator's roar faded, Paul could hear his brothers' voices again.

"Help us!" William shouted.

"We're coming!" Paul shouted back. He could see a flash of white in the dark water beyond the little island. As he stared at it, the shape made sense. Somehow, they had managed to capsize the bateau. He lowered his voice. "Is there some way to scare the alligator off?"

Lily was shaking her head as she used her paddle to turn the pirogue at an angle. They drifted to a stop and floated, motionless, on the dark water. Lily pointed. "See that pile of grass and branches?"

Paul followed her gesture, peering into the shadows. "You mean at the base of those tupelo gums?"

Lily nodded. "Yes. It's her nest. She still has eggs in there. She must have or she wouldn't be defending it like this."

Paul looked up at his brothers. Even from here he could see that their faces were strained and pale beneath the lumpy swellings of mosquito bites. Mark looked like he wanted to cry. William looked angry. The alligator snapped her massive jaws and swung her tail menacingly.

Paul knew a hundred stories about alligators, and they all came rushing into his mind. The big animals often killed their prey by drowning it. They did not chew, but swallowed their meals whole, jerking their heads back and forth to tear their prey into pieces.

Jedediah had once told him a story about a 'gator carrying off a four-month-old calf. Paul had never believed the story could be true—until now. This alligator was big enough to kill a lamb or a calf.

"Help us!" William screamed, facing the pirogue. "Paul, do something!"

Paul felt his heart sinking. He had been so happy when he had realized the distant sound was his brothers' voices. Now, a cold sheen of sweat coated his face. What could he possibly do? For an eerie second he imagined one of his brothers falling, tumbling to earth, suddenly within reach of the huge, long, sharp teeth.

The alligator suddenly leaped upward, throwing her weight on her muscular tail. She balanced just long enough to snap her jaws shut less than an arm's length from William's foot.

"Help me!" William shrieked at Paul. Then he swore, demanding that Mark move higher in the vines.

"I can't go any farther," Mark yelled back at him.

"Tell them to quiet themselves," Lily said to Paul.

He shrugged, staring helplessly as his brothers struggled to climb upward. The alligator was maddened, twisting, and roaring her throaty call.

"Tell them!" Lily insisted.

Paul was certain William and Mark would never hear him, but he glanced at Lily's fierce frown and put his hands around his mouth. "Be quiet!" He waited a few seconds, then tried again. His brothers ignored him.

Lily scowled. "If they won't stop yelling, there is nothing anyone can do for them."

Paul glanced from her to his brothers. "Be still!" he screamed. "Quiet! William! Stop making noise!" For a second, William didn't react. But then he fell silent, glaring at Paul.

"Do something!" Mark shouted over the roaring of the enraged alligator.

William began screaming and shouting again. Mark started up as well, this time yelling for her to go get real help.

"Make them stop or I will leave now," Lily said.

Paul looked at her, wondering if she meant it. She might. His brothers had been merciless in mocking her, and he knew she hated them. He watched the twins for a few seconds, remembering all the times they had arranged elaborate tricks that had made him feel helpless and weak.

Out of the corner of his eye, Paul saw Lily lift the paddle. Her face was serious, almost grave. She was not making a dramatic gesture. She really meant to leave his brothers right where they were.

Paul twisted around to Mark and William. "Be still!" Half standing in the pirogue, Paul screamed the words, ignoring his painfully rasping throat. The pirogue swayed in the water, canting to one side, and he sat back down.

Lily back-paddled a few strokes, turning the pirogue around. The alligator's roaring faded suddenly. "If you can't be quiet, I'm leaving."

"What?" William shouted in the unexpected quiet. His voice rebounded from a thick stand of cypress.

"Get hold of yourself, William," Mark exploded. "They'll leave us here."

"I will leave," Lily said, lifting her chin, "if you do one more stupid thing."

Paul stared at her. Her head was high, and she raised the paddle to show she meant it. The twins exchanged a look, but neither said anything.

An odd, high-pitched grunting startled Paul. He stared at the alligator. "Why is she doing that?"

Lily did not answer. Her eyes were fixed on the alligator.

"Does that mean she's calming down?" Paul whispered.

Lily still said nothing. When he leaned forward to whisper the question a second time, she made an impatient slashing motion with her right hand.

Paul turned to stare at the alligator. Her huge jaws were shut now, and the arch in her back had flattened. She was looking at the mound of rotted limbs and leaves she stood beside.

Chapter Thirteen

Lily knew Paul was staring at her intently, but she refused to meet his eyes. She was considering an idea that was so dangerous it frightened her, but she couldn't come up with a better one.

"What's that noise?"

Lily glanced at Paul, his voice pulling her out of her thoughts even though she had not really understood him. His swollen face made him look miserable, like a child who had been weeping. "We might be able to get them away," Lily told him.

Paul's eyes widened. "How?"

Lily nodded toward the nest. "That is the sound of her babies. They are hatching."

Paul turned his head back toward the nest. "That's why she won't leave?"

Lily barely nodded, her thoughts already racing again. If the alligator was a good mother, they stood a chance. The alligator bellowed again, lurched back on her tail once more, and snapped, this time falling back with a mouthful of leaves. William groaned, then shouted at Paul. The alligator lunged again.

"William, shut your mouth," Lily heard Mark say. Then he began talking to William in a low voice that Lily could not hear well enough to understand. Lily waited, watching the alligator gradually lose interest in the whispering boys above her as the sound of her own young once more entranced her.

"What can we do?" Paul asked quietly.

Lily focused on him once more. "If she is a good mother, she will help her babies to the water."

"Really? How?" Paul looked back toward the big alligator, and Lily marveled that he did not already know how. Lily opened her own mouth wide, then closed it slowly and gently.

"In her *mouth*?"

The look of amazement on Paul's face was almost enough to make Lily laugh. "But of course," she told him. "How else?"

"But what about her teeth?" Paul asked.

Lily could not suppress a chuckle. "Your own mother has teeth, doesn't she?"

Paul looked aside, and Lily reached out to touch his shoulder. "I will explain it to you, then I want you to tell them." She jutted her chin out, indicating the little island where William and Mark waited, finally quiet, their eyes on her and Paul.

"Soon, the babies will cry louder," Lily said. She had seen alligators hatching several times. Once, she and Augustin had climbed a tree to watch. She knew what would happen and about how long it would take. But she had no idea how the alligator would react to being interrupted.

"Look!" Paul was tugging at her sleeve.

The alligator had begun digging. Lily leaned toward Paul. "She is moving the nest aside so her children can come out now. We are lucky."

Paul looked puzzled. "Lucky?"

Lily nodded. "They have probably been singing to her for hours. Perhaps they are very close to hatching."

Paul rubbed his swollen cheek. "How long will it take?"

Lily shrugged. "I think it can be different each time."

That seemed to satisfy Paul, at least for the moment. Lily took advantage of his silence to scan the channel that bordered this side of the island.

The channel was so narrow that Lily bit her lip. If it were wider, her decisions would be easier. Then she could be sure of having enough room to turn the pirogue. As it was, there was no way to be sure the channel went on, and she could not be positive that if she had to turn around, there would be enough room to do it.

Lily drew in a sharp breath, imagining for a second what might happen. If the alligator charged them and she could not get the pirogue away from the bank, she might leap into the boat with them. If that happened, she might kill them all.

"I see one," Paul whispered.

"There are eggs in the leaves!" Mark called softly.

Lily nodded and pressed one finger to her lips, hoping Mark could see her well enough to understand. Paul reacted angrily, shaking his head and gesturing at his brother to be silent.

"If they are quiet, she might forget they're up

there," Lily whispered. "The only chance we have is to wait until she is busy carrying her babies to the water. Then, if your brothers can get down quickly enough and run to the pirogue, we might all get away."

"What if the alligator chases them?"

Lily could only shrug. "She will, if she sees them. Perhaps they can outrun her. They cannot outswim her."

Paul was quiet for another moment, and she could see he understood what she was planning. He was scanning the bank of the channel, as she had done. Then he looked at her again. "Where?"

Lily hesitated. William and Mark would have to climb down, then run. If she picked a place too far from the nest, they might not make it. But if she chose a place too close . . . "It depends upon where the mother goes into the water."

Paul looked at the alligator again, and Lily followed his gaze. The big animal was still digging gently at her nesting material. The babies' high-pitched cries were getting louder.

"Perhaps we should just wait," Lily said.

Paul shook his head. "I thought of that. But look

at them." He indicated his brothers clinging to the vines. Mark was slumped forward. William kept hitching himself higher, then sliding back down. They were weak and close to exhaustion.

Lily nodded. "You are right. If they fall, she will be upon them instantly."

"How much longer do we have to wait?" Paul asked.

"We will have to wait for the right time," Lily said. "Once she finds an easy path, she will use it again and again."

"I should tell them," Paul said, indicating his brothers.

Lily looked at William and Mark. They were clutching at the thick vines, watching the alligator over their shoulders. "Tell them," Lily said. "But if they start to yell again, they will only remind her they are up there."

Paul nodded and sat up straighter. He shouted for his brothers to listen without speaking. Then he quickly explained, adding that Lily would be the one to decide where they would meet on the bank, and when.

Lily watched the alligator the whole time Paul was yelling to his brothers. The big animal did not stop her digging and still seemed oblivious to William and Mark. The pirogue was far enough away that the sound of Paul's voice was no more a threat to the alligator than the intermittent bird-calls that pierced the heavy air.

Lily rolled her shawl into a tight bundle and used it to pad her shoulders against the side of the pirogue.

"How much longer, do you think?" Paul asked her.

She shrugged and leaned back. "I hope not too long. My father will never forgive me."

Paul looked so miserable, she was sorry she had said it, even though she knew it might almost be true. Maman would be upset about all the same things Papa would be upset about, Lily knew. And then Maman would notice her mud-stained skirt and blouse. Lily sighed. Her parents were going to have twenty things to be angry about before it was all over.

Paul slid off the bench and turned to stretch out his legs. He leaned back and closed his eyes. Lily could not tell if he had fallen asleep. She knew he had to be exhausted. He could not have slept much sitting in a tree for two nights.

The time crept past, hanging as heavily as the curtains of grayish moss that shrouded the trees. Birds called overhead, and there was a constant humming of insects. Lily caught herself staring at nothing several times before the alligator finally lifted her head and stopped her ponderous digging.

Lily watched her take a few steps forward, then incline her long snout, opening her mouth. "Paul!" She nudged him.

"What?"

"She is about to carry her babies, I think. I want you to get in front."

He stared at her, a puzzled look on his face. "Why?"

"With your brothers' weight added, I will be able to turn the pirogue better from the back," she hissed at him, trying to remember that it was not his fault he had never learned so many simple things.

Paul awkwardly made his way around her, and the pirogue rocked on the water.

"Be careful," Lily warned.

Paul apologized under his breath, settling himself

on the narrow plank she had been sitting upon as she stood, feet wide apart, until he had stopped moving. Then she made her way to the stern and arranged her skirt, lowering herself onto the rear bench. Then they both turned to face the little island.

Lily straightened up to see better, letting out a nervous sigh. The alligator was dipping her head lower. All at once she opened her jaws and made a deft scooping motion. Then she backed up a step or two before angling off to one side.

Paul turned toward Lily. "She's got one in her mouth."

Lily nodded, putting a finger to her lips. He wasn't talking loudly enough for his voice to reach the alligator, but she wanted to concentrate. She held her breath, hoping the *cocodrie* would decide to carry her babies to the far side of the hummock of ground—the farther the better.

Lily could not look away, even for a moment. So much depended on what the mother 'gator did next. If she went to the far side, she'd be facing away from them and she might not even see the pirogue approaching. But if she came this way, it was going to make things much harder, maybe even impossible. Lily took a deep breath, waiting as the alligator backed away from her nest and hesitated, then started off at an angle.

Lily exhaled slowly, ignoring Paul's eager glances. The 'gator's path was neither directly toward the pirogue nor away from it. Lily waved her arms over her head to get William's and Mark's attention. When she was sure they were looking at her, she made an exaggerated gesture, covering her mouth with both hands. Then, hoping they had understood and would stay quiet, she picked up her paddle.

"What are you doing?" Paul gripped the edge of the bench. "Should I tell them to get ready?"

Lily shook her head. "Not yet." Ignoring his questioning stare, she lifted the paddle, then slid it into the water so gently that there was no sound at all. Maneuvering backward, she found another narrow channel that veered toward the alligator's nest.

Paddling slowly and smoothly, she started up it, her eyes flickering back and forth between the narrow channel of dark water and the alligator. The moment the big animal turned to come back to her nest, Lily back-paddled, bringing the pirogue to a drifting stop.

"Hold still," she whispered to Paul. They weren't really any closer than they had been, but she was afraid the alligator would notice them now that they had moved. It took very little to provoke a female alligator with babies into an attack.

Lily glanced at Paul's brothers. They were still, looking down at the nest as the alligator came back toward them. Lily wondered how long they had been clinging to the vines, if they had spent the whole night up there.

"She's going to go back to the same place," Paul said quietly.

Lily nodded. "If she does it once more, we'll try to get your brothers into the pirogue. Once we get close, move as far forward as you can. Then sit as still as stone and tell your brothers to as well."

As she spoke, the alligator reached into the leaves and pulled another hatchling free of the mound. Her jaw slack, the big animal turned and headed away again.

Lily stood up and waved her arms over her head, then made an insistent motion downward. The instant she saw Paul's brothers start to descend, she sat down and picked up the paddle. Leaning into every stroke, her eyes fixed on the retreating alligator, Lily made her pirogue skim over the dark water. She could feel her own pulse at the base of her throat. It was now or never.

Chapter Fourteen

Paul sat still, his hands extended, clasping the sides of the pirogue. He could feel the boat moving forward in overlapping, lungelike spurts, timed with Lily's paddling. He glanced back over his shoulder. She was bending almost double, reaching so far forward that her arms were completely extended, her bare feet braced against the bottom of the pirogue.

Paul looked toward the island. His brothers were halfway down—William moving faster than Mark. The alligator seemed not to have noticed anything was going on behind her. Paul leaned forward, trying to center his weight. He could hear Lily breathing hard as she paddled, but he did not turn to look at her. He could only stare at his brothers' slow, downward climb, and pray.

William hit the ground and stumbled, his feet tangled in the creeper vines. A second later Mark was also on the ground. Paul knew exactly what was happening to them. Their legs had cramped like his had.

William rolled onto his belly and tried to stand, falling once more. He was clearly panicked, jerking at the vines like a trapped animal, glancing every few seconds toward the alligator.

Paul raised his arms and waved frantically, trying to get William to see how close they were. In seconds, the pirogue would be alongside the bank.

Abruptly, William lifted his head and focused on Paul. "Help!" he shouted. "Paul, help me!"

Paul shook his fist at his brother, desperate to silence him. Instantly, William clapped one hand over his mouth, realizing what he had done. But it was too late. The alligator had been standing at the water's edge, opposite her nest. Now she turned, enraged and bellowing.

"Run!" Paul screamed.

William tried to stand, but the creeper vines brought him down again, and he thrashed sideways. Mark was in even worse shape. He lay on his back, one knee drawn up against his chest, his face contorted in pain.

"Run!" Paul screamed again.

"I can't!" Mark groaned. "I can't even stand up!"

Lily turned the pirogue sharply. Paul lost his handhold and pitched to his left, scraping his ribs against the side of the boat. He shoved himself straight, then fell again as she maneuvered around a sunken log.

Paul managed to right himself once more and looked up, fear tightening his throat. His brothers were both still caught in the vines. They looked like wounded men, half standing, then falling again. Paul remembered the awful cramps and the strange numbness that had crippled him at first.

The alligator was rushing toward William and Mark, her tail slashing the grass as she came. Lily brought the pirogue around hard, and Paul was thrown to the side again, but he dragged himself up, his eyes on his brothers. "Get up!" he shouted. "Run! You have to!" He clenched his teeth. They had gotten themselves so tangled in the vines and they were so weak, he wasn't sure they could free themselves in time.

The pirogue slowed as it turned, bumping up against the muddy bank. "Hurry!" Lily yelled. Then she dropped her voice. "Paul, here, take this!"

Paul turned to see her dropping the paddle, fumbling through the food bag. An instant later, she tossed him a knife. He caught it and wrenched around, standing up as the pirogue tipped and swayed beneath him.

"Cut them free!" Lily shouted, and he could hear the desperation in her voice.

An echoing bellow rattled Paul's nerves as he stepped ashore. The alligator was slowing, her back humped up and her terrible jaws open now. Mark was closest, and Paul sprinted toward him. Slashing at the vines, Paul managed to drag Mark to his feet and, together, Mark's arm around his shoulders, they staggered toward the pirogue. William was still struggling to get to his feet, but he seemed, at last, to understand he had to stay quiet.

His heart pounding inside his chest, Paul lifted Mark over the side of the boat, half dropping him in the bow. Mark sprawled, crying out as Paul whirled back around, expecting to see the alligator attacking William.

What he saw gave him a glimmer of hope. The

alligator had rushed back to her nest and was facing William, still making the terrible sound that seemed to shake the very air.

"Paul, don't go back!" Lily screamed. "She'll kill you!"

Paul clutched the knife and ran toward William, curving outward to avoid the nest. The alligator bellowed and twisted around to face him, following his progress.

Paul sprinted, his fear strengthening his legs. The alligator advanced, stiff legged, her jaws open wide. Then she turned toward her nest again, her whole body rigid with rage, clacking her jaws shut on empty air.

"Cocodrie!"

Paul turned. It was Lily, standing on the bank, her paddle in her hands, waving it over her head and screaming at the top of her lungs. The alligator turned toward her.

Paul ran to his brother. "William was sitting upright, his eyes wide. Dragging in sobbing breaths, Paul cut at the vines wrapped around his brother's legs and ankles. He could still hear Lily shouting a frenzy of French at the alligator. He was afraid to look.

Dragging William to his feet, Paul started back toward the pirogue.

"Look out," Mark shrieked.

Paul looked up to see the alligator had noticed them. She was turning away from Lily and coming back toward her nest. In the loose leaves, Paul could see the eggs, most of them with a tiny blunt snout showing out one end.

Zigzagging, pulling William along, Paul went backward, putting the nest between them and the alligator. Reluctant to trample her own babies, the big animal stopped and looked back toward Lily. She hobbled forward, brandishing the paddle and shrieking again. Paul waited until the alligator turned to face her, then he dragged William into a stumbling run.

William fell to his knees, and Paul yanked him up, forcing him to keep going. Glancing at the alligator, he saw she had stopped at the bank where the pirogue had been. "Paul! This way!"

He let go of William and whirled around. Lily was paddling ferociously along the narrow channel, maneuvering the pirogue like a songbird darting through dense branches. Paul understood instantly what she was trying to do. She had led the alligator to the edge of the water, then paddled away, leaving her standing there. By moving the pirogue she was giving them a clear path and a second chance.

Paul grabbed William again, clutching the knife in his free hand. Backing up, dragging William with him, Paul began to close the distance to the boat. The alligator faced Paul from across the little island now, her menacing calls grating at his nerves, battering at his courage. His legs were shaking, but he still felt strangely strong. William was leaning heavily on his shoulder. The alligator's threatening roars became sharper and louder, and Paul looked up to see her coming toward them again. He turned and ran, pulling William along as fast as he could. As they got close to the pirogue, Paul could hear Mark and Lily shouting encouragement.

"I don't want to die!" William gasped, twisting his arm out of Paul's grasp just as they reached the bank. He fell, floundering on the grass as Paul tried frantically to get him back on his feet. Glancing back at the alligator, Paul saw that this time their luck had run out. She was not pausing at her nest again. She was coming straight toward them.

Fear made it impossible for Paul to scream or even to think. He bent down, dragging at William's arm.

"Come on!" Mark was yelling. Lily's stream of French was fierce and loud, and Paul knew she was threatening the alligator. He turned and stumbled when he realized how close she was behind them. Spinning back around, he dropped the knife long enough to shove William forward. He fell across the pirogue, kicking his legs as he tried to right himself. Paul turned back to grab the knife and scrambled sideways, jumping in just behind Mark. William was still floundering, shouting angrily.

"William! Get in!" Lily screamed as the bellowing roar of the alligator was suddenly right beside them. Paul wrenched around to see the animal rushing forward, her jaws wide, then closing on his brother's extended legs.

William's agonized scream made Paul clamber upright, twisting back to see the alligator's scaled back just inches from his face. There was blood oozing from William's leg, and the alligator was lunging toward him again.

Without thinking, Paul thrust the knife upright into the animal's mouth. He shoved the blade upward as Mark managed to pull William into the boat.

"Hold on!" Lily warned.

Paul let go of the knife the moment the pirogue slid backward. He saw it fall free and drop to the ground as the alligator shook her head.

"Sit still and stay in the center," Paul yelled at his brothers. Mark managed to position himself as Lily fought to back-paddle along the narrow channel. William was sobbing, his hands tight around his bloody leg. Paul reached back and held him upright. The pirogue balanced itself in the water and began to turn more sharply.

The alligator plunged into the water behind them, but Lily had the boat nearly turned by the time she attacked the heavy cypress wood of the pirogue. Paul heard the ugly gnashing of her teeth as she grunted and gave her raging call once more.

Lily was paddling for all their lives now, and Paul watched as she leaned first to one side, then the other, to see the way ahead. Without a single false move, she settled into a rhythm of long, back-bending strokes. Paul looked back, his breath coming in ragged gasps.

The alligator had given up. He saw her climbing out of the channel and making her way back to her nest.

"William is hurt pretty bad," Paul said. He pulled his shirt off and began tearing it into strips to make a bandage.

"You saved us!" Mark said between shuddering breaths.

"Lily is the one who saved us," Paul corrected him. "She saved us all."

Chapter Fifteen

Lily kept paddling, even though her arms were aching. She wanted to clear the edge of the swamp and be back on Bayou Teche as soon as she could. The pirogue was heavy and clumsy as she wove through the mosaic of land and water. It was hard.

To make matters worse, William was lying down and he kept wrenching himself from side to side as Paul wound the long strips of cloth around his ragged wounds. Mark was in the bow, staring straight ahead without speaking.

Lily tried to imagine what Monsieur Courville was going to say. His sons were alive, but they were all hurt. Now that Paul had pulled his shirt off, Lily could see huge, blue-black bruises on his chest and back. His legs were probably worse. Mark's hands were scratched and bloody, and one of his shoes was missing. William's wounds were bleeding terribly, and he was pale and obviously weak.

Lily could only keep paddling. Paul held the waterskin for each of his brothers, then asked Lily if he could give them corn bread as well. She nodded, wondering if Maman would mind if most of her food ended up in Courville stomachs.

William's sobbing subsided slowly until he lay still and closed his eyes. Paul looked up, and Lily met his gaze.

"Is he all right?" she asked.

Paul hesitated. "I think so. How long will it take to get him home?"

Lily narrowed her eyes, staring as William shoved himself back into a sitting position. He glanced at her, then looked away. "We never meant any harm," he said.

Lily stared at him. "Then what exactly did you mean?"

William stammered, then fell silent. "We just wanted to scare him. It was supposed to be funny."

He closed his eyes for a moment, his face contorted with pain.

"All your tricks are mean," Paul said. "And I never tell Father because I know you'll just play more tricks if I do."

"It wasn't just me. Mark—" William said.

"It was your idea," Mark interrupted. "All the tricks are your ideas." He shook his head. "I've just been stupid enough to go along with them."

"You could have killed Paul," Lily accused.

William looked away.

"You could have killed him and Mark and me," she told him. "That is what my poor parents are probably thinking this moment. That I am dead."

Mark frowned. "They worry about you in the swamp?"

Lily glared angrily at him. "Of course they do. Do you think my father sends his daughter out alone to help boys who have never done anything but insult her and mock her?" On the last word, Lily caught her breath, fighting tears. She refused to cry now.

Mark had lowered his head. "I'm sorry, Lily."

"Why did you do it?" Lily lifted the paddle from

the water, letting the pirogue drift. She looked from William to Mark, then back, meeting their eyes until they both looked away. Then she lowered her paddle back into the water and began to row.

As she maneuvered her pirogue, Lily knew all three of them were looking at her. She kept her eyes averted, leaning to look past them at the narrow waterway she was trying to follow. She could see Paul nudging William, but refused to look directly at them.

"I apologize," William finally muttered.

Lily pretended not to hear him.

"I'm sorry," he started over. "I never meant for anyone to get hurt."

Mark sat silently for a full minute after William was finished. Then he lifted his chin. "Thank you for helping us. You saved our lives."

Lily finally turned, her eyes meeting Paul's as she answered Mark. "You can thank your brother. If he hadn't been lost with you, I would not have come at all." There was a silence, then Mark turned to look out over the water, and William lay back down. Lily fell back to paddling.

Using the glitter of the late afternoon sun to guide

her toward the Teche, Lily managed to come out from beneath the canopy of trees almost within sight of LaSalle's landing. She handed Paul the paddle and rubbed at her arms, trying to ease the aching that had spread from her fingertips to her shoulders.

Paul managed to keep the pirogue more or less straight, and Lily was grateful for the opportunity to rest. She ate the last of the corn bread and a little of the fish. When she noticed Mark staring at her, she offered him some of the pork and rice. Paul and William joined in, and for a few minutes they floated aimlessly as the food disappeared. Then Paul began to paddle again.

As they made slow progress upstream, the sun was hot. William moaned and shifted on the hard wood bottom of the pirogue. Lily rolled her shawl and tucked it beneath his head. He opened his eyes. "Thank you."

Lily started to look away, but he reached up and caught her hand. "I mean it. Thank you."

Lily nodded, pulling her hand free.

"There's Father with John and Mr. Thomas," Mark called out.

Lily looked up. He was right. The bateau was

coming fast—both John and Mr. Thomas were rowing. Paul caught Lily's eye and gestured. There, on the other side of the bayou, was a smaller bateau that held one man: her father. He stood, waving his arms and shouting her name. Lily felt her heart lift. He might be angry later, but for now, he was overjoyed she was alive and well.

"Paul!" Monsieur Courville was shouting. "Are you and your brothers all right?"

Paul passed the paddle to Lily so he could stand up. "William's hurt. Not too badly," he shouted back. "If it weren't for Lily, we'd all be dead."

Within minutes, Lily's pirogue was flanked on either side by the flat-bottomed bateaus. Her father embraced her and helped move William to his father's boat. Mark and Paul managed the switch without assistance.

"What the devil were you three doing out there?" Monsieur Courville demanded. "And where is my bateau?"

His usually pink face was florid beneath the glaring sun. Mark and Paul exchanged a look. "Ask William," Paul said evenly, and Lily heard the quiet self-assurance in his voice. Monsieur Courville heard it too, and he looked startled, then turned to William and demanded an explanation of what had happened.

As Papa tied Lily's pirogue to the stern of the bateau, Lily glanced at Paul to find him looking straight at her. "Thank you again, Lily," he said loudly.

As Papa began to pole the bateau into a wide arc, John and Mr. Thomas turned. Monsieur Courville, his hands resting lightly on Paul's shoulders, looked up. They all waved a farewell, and Monsieur Courville shouted his thanks as the distance between the boats increased.

Lily waved to Paul, then waited for her father to speak. He poled for a long time in silence, then finally faced her. "Paul behaved as a gentleman?"

Lily nodded. "And he made sure his father thanked me."

Papa looked into her eyes. "Perhaps he is your friend."

Lily hugged her father, and he stroked her tangled hair. "Your Maman is going to be very relieved when she sees you. Promise me you will never do anything like this again."

Lily leaned against her father for a moment, feeling

safe again. "I promise. I am so sorry, Papa."

He looked at her, smiling. "You are alive. It has ended well. That is enough for me."

Lily lay her head on his shoulder for a moment, then drew back, picking up her own paddle. "We should hurry," she said. "Maman will be waiting."